THE TALES OF OLLUNDRA

AN ANTHOLOGY OF THE WORLD OF OLLUNDRA

CREATED BY CRAIG TEAL

Copyright © 2016 by Composite Games Limited

First Published in 2016 by Composite Games Limited

The Chronicles of Ollundra intellectual property is to be identified as property of Composite Games Limited in accordance of with the copyright, designs and patents act 1988

All rights reserved. No part of this publication me be reproduced, stored in a system, or transmitted, in any form or by any means without the prior written permission of the publisher, nor be otherwise circulated in any for of binding or cover other than in it is published and without similar condition being imposed on the subsequent purchaser.

ISBN-10: 1537278096

All characters in this publication are fictitious and any persons, living or dead, is purely coincidental

Cover Art by Joel Lagerwall

Published by Composite Games Limited

Composite Games Limited
12 Ridgewood Avenue
Doncaster
England
DN3 2JP

Contents

Foreword	6
An Introduction to Ollundra	10
Sins of the Father	15
The Fall and Redeption of Davaldion	87
Of Mice and Dragons	151
Withertale	195
The Wolves Guardian	262
Acknowledgements	304

Foreword

Being a writer and reader rather a gamer, when I was first approached as a creative consultant for Composite Games I was not sure what to expect. Another problem for me was that fantasy is not my preferred genre (although, like most people, I am a massive Harry Potter fan) so getting to grips with the setting for the Chronicles of Ollundra took some getting used to. However, when Craig, the creative director and creator of The Chronicles of Ollundra, approached me about doing a companion book to tie in with the release of the game, I felt my feet were on more comfortable, even ground.

And so the task began. We already had a couple of writers on board, but an advert was put out to see if anyone else was interested in writing a story for us, based around the setting of Ollundra. Writers were given a brief to follow; although we wanted writers to be as creative as possible, we still wanted the stories to have some sort of consistency with each other so as not to confuse and muddle the world we were creating.

It has to be said, the response was delightfully surprising. Many people from around the world, both professional and amateur writers, showed a lot of interest in the project and took up the mantle. After much sifting through, six stories were chosen to be included in the anthology. Competition was fierce, but myself (as editor and proofreader) and Craig feel we have chosen the strongest stories.

Many thanks should be given to the six writers – Josh Vogt, Craig Teal, Mary Hukel, Péter Holló-Vaskó, Nikki Yager and Katrina Werline who have all individually worked so hard and, as a result, have managed to capture the atmosphere of Ollundra and developed it in such a way that they bring the whole setting to life.

I believe that this book makes a great companion to the world we are trying to make, and on behalf of Composite Games hope you will enjoy this anthology as much as I have enjoyed being a part of its creation.

Ali Jennings 2015

An Introduction to Ollundra

The world of Ollundra was created by Craig Teal and was initially intended to provide a setting for a tabletop roleplaying game that was being produced by Composite Games Limited.

However it was later decided that Composite Games would produce a fantasy anthology based around and introducing key characters in Ollundra to help introduce people to the setting.

The World

Ollundra is an ancient and magic world that has been the battle ground for many wars, the last of which resulted in a worldwide cataclysm that rocked the world and shattered the empires of old.

Now over a thousand years later the decedents of the survivors are only just beginning to return to the grandeur they once took for granted so many years ago.

However, deep within the cracks of the world an ancient evil has been plotting the return of their fallen master.

The world of Ollundra is split into four continents, with the continent of Hesperia being the focus of this anthology.

Hesperia itself was once home to a great empire, though the cataclysm has reduced this fraction of its former size with the remnants of the empire now standing as individual kingdoms with their own rulers and alliances.

The continent itself is home to a varied amount of people and races with humans being the most numerous, followed by elves, Halflings, dwarves, shadelings, fey and a multitude of other races.

Ten Important Things about Ollundra

1) The four continents of Ollundra are not equally populated with a large jungle covered continent to the south of Hesperia largely uncharted.

2) The fallen continent of Umbravi was abandoned long ago to the ruinous powers that dwelt there with only a small elvish enclave remaining.

3) Khellus Blackheart is not Khellus's real name and a few believe he was given the title blackheart as he has no soul.

4) The Morningstar is a revered demigod that is said to only return when the darkness between worlds returns.

5) Ironcliffe is the current capital of the remnants of the Ashalian Empire.

6) The Ashalian Empire now only consists of the Kingdoms of Tradoria, Assillia and Caria.

7) The entity that destroyed Corona was not the first of the dark elder gods to return.

8) Damitri's father D'car was the first of the Darkling's to break the hold of the dark god that ensnared him.

9) At the heart of Hesperia lies the Elven lands, no one but the elves are admitted entrance. With all trade being done at the five city states that surround their lands.

10) Rumour has it that the entity that seeks the Morningstar was not created by the Sleeper and is alien to the world of Ollundra.

A World of Adventure Awaits

We hope you enjoy these stories and we look forward to sharing more tales of Ollundra with you in the future.

Sins of the Father

By

Josh Vogt

Chapter 1

The crimson city of Belladain sat in the middle of a long valley between two opposing mountain ranges, like a ruby cupped in the palms and offered as a gift. Khellus figured the trade city's stature was fitting enough for its darker name, Jewel of Thorns. Beautiful, with its elegant towers, verdant gardens, and silver-etched gates. Yet as many would be invaders and rulers had discovered over the centuries, should you try to snatch it up or grip it too tight the blood would flow.

He'd been there before, six years earlier. Part of a retinue ensuring an ambassador's protection during a diplomatic meeting with the barbarian merchant clans from the West. Now he returned on a mission of death.

Squeezing his knees, Khellus urged his chestnut mare into a trot toward the western gate. The horse nickered as it clopped along, Khellus riding easy in the saddle. Wearing simple black leathers and a white cloth tunic, grey cloak devoid of any royal insignia, he might've looked like any commoner but for the twin long blades strapped to his broad shoulders. Still, any person foolish enough to ride the Bloodrose Road without

armaments deserved what they got.

He analysed the outer walls for flaws and climbing routes. He marked the locations of lower grates, where several sewers and rivers sometimes indistinguishable snaked out from under the buttresses. Cold blue mage fires burned in watchtowers ringing the city, while webs of buttery faelights clung to a few of the larger buildings at the city's centre, where the Trade Justices held court.

Every obvious point of ingress or egress looked carefully

guarded, even the water grates. As expected. Belladain thrived on the exchange of goods and coin within its bounds and kept its secrets as close to its jealous bosom as possible.

Did Abrodail still dwell there? What might've become of her? Still working in that tavern? Dead of random alley thuggery? Or had she perhaps fallen in with a better lot? Perhaps he should've left a few coins along with the note…

Khellus brought his focus back to the task at hand as he approached the gates. He blended in well enough with the other travellers and caravans crowding the area and soon passed through. If anything, Belladain had only grown more crowded and boisterous in the years he'd been gone. All manner of man and beast packed the winding streets, filling the air with the stench of civilisation and roar of commerce. He guided his mount through the throngs. The turmoil wouldn't ebb with the encroaching twilight, but would just be replaced by another sort of revelry involving drink, deviousness, and all manners of debauchery.

Khellus's gaze lingered on a woman slumped in a domicile threshold. Eyes shut, mouth gaping, one would've thought her dead but for the occasional twitch of legs under her skirt. Streaks of platinum-blonde hair coursed through her otherwise black tresses, and blood seeped from cracks in her fingernails. Those combined with the leg twitches were signs of rampant *dravillish* use.

He let his gaze slide past her and oriented himself. Dravillish was just one of the many pernicious drugs Belladain dealt in below all its other transactions of silk, spices, flesh, and soul. She looked like she'd crashed. He knew the energy and focus the drug promised was false. That eventually you'd end up as this woman had, with mind-wrenching exhaustion. One more addict didn't concern him. Even though she could easily slip into a life threatening stupor if she couldn't replenish her supply. She'd made her choices in life and now paid the price. He had enough of his own to pay to take on anyone else's debts.

To meet his current obligation, he needed to find his contact, get the salient details, finish the job, and slip out of the city before the blood dried on the stones. Quick, quiet, and yet effective in sending a message - king's orders.

He chose an inn at random and paid for a three night stay, though he intended just one. He had his horse stabled and tipped the muck boy a half-copper to ensure the feed had no bugs in it. As night spread a sable blanket across the city and its conjured lights blurred the stars, Khellus strode off for the nearest marketplace.

He found the proper shop an hour later. The engraved board above the door displayed *T'ings and F'ings*. He allowed a small chuckle at the crude gutter speak which also served as code among many royal agents across the kingdom. He ducked into the alley alongside the establishment, which stunk of piss and offal. Odd patterns of soot and the occasional streak of dried blood marked the stones all over. Tucking his gloves into his belt, Khellus clambered to the roof, picked the lock on the waiting hatch, and dropped into a lightless upper storeroom.

He prowled through stacks of dusty crates and scattered stock until he found another door. Using a tiny vial from a pouch on his belt, he dripped oil onto the hinges, and then opened it, revealing the living quarters behind the shop. He detected a subtle scent of lemons as he slipped though the doorway.

The shop owner, hefty men, with a permanent flush to his pale neck and cheeks, sat at a table lit by several large candles. He dithered over a simple dinner of roasted dog flesh and herb-rubbed bread. A ledger lay open on the table beside the meal, and he ticked off entries with an inked quill as he picked at his food.

Khellus studied him for a few minutes, noting the sweat gleaming on his bald head and the slightest quiver to his fingers as he wrote. Then the assassin descended the stairs and leant against the wall directly behind the man. To his left, a wooden slat door closed off what he assumed to be a closet, while another stood half-open to reveal a bedroom with armoire and feather-stuffed mattress. A third doorway, blocked by a silk curtain, led into the shop front.

He waited until just the right moment, as the shop keeper took another bite of bread. Devils above and below, he loved this part of the work.

He cleared his throat.

Crumbs spewed. Meal and book went flying as the man shoved the table away, spinning as he rose, quill thrust out like a dagger. His chest heaved and the bloodshot whites of his eyes showed as he staggered for balance.

"Easy, Dolomun" Khellus rumbled. "Your heart isn't allowed to fail until you've given your report. Then you can have all the spasms you want."

"Khellus?" Dolomun squinted and blinked in relief. "You're early."

Khellus scowled at having his name spoken aloud. In a land of unending suspicion and scryers-for-hire, even the tiniest slip of the tongue could unravel the most tight-knit operation. He waited while

Dolomun recovered the scattered food and sat on shaky legs. The pulse along his throat remained rapid.

"Schedules are for those who want to be caught," Khellus said, keeping his poise neutral. "When your arrival is expected, your enemies can take advantage of punctuality."

"Yes, well, if you're done with your fun, perhaps we can see to our business and I can get back to my peaceful evening?"

"Please."

Dolomun crossed beefy arms. "Your services are no longer required."

Khellus raised eyebrows. "Truly? When High King Devdan sent me here, it seemed my orders were rather straightforward and urgent."

"Things can change drastically in a week or two. The contract is ended. I was told to inform you as soon as you arrived so you wouldn't errantly slaughter a true servant of the king"

Khellus straightened. "So Wescel Asmoran is considered a true servant, is he?"

"New evidence has come to light. The crimes for which he was to be removed have been revealed to be part of a conspiracy to mar his reputation and instigate just such a removal." Dolomun jutted his chin at Khellus. "If you'd killed him, another noble would be quick to take his place, one tied tight to the Bloodrose's coin purses rather than the king's."

"I see." Khellus mumbled as he stared into space contemplating his next move noting, in the corner of his eye, how Dolomun fidgeted. His gaze shot back to Dolomun and he shrugged. "I'm afraid I take my orders straight from the king's mouth, not from a secondary such as yourself."

"But I received directions from the High Magus," Dolomun said. "It took them great cost and effort to send the message across this distance"

"I'll be sure to inform the king he needs better channels of communication. In the meantime, you can tell your new friends they need to work on giving you better cover stories." Khellus headed for the stairs he'd snuck down, and then paused. "On second thought, I'll deliver the news myself."

He drew a blade as he whirled and plunged it through the thin slats of the closet door. It struck soft flesh on the other side, and a scream wrenched the air. Khellus yanked the sword free, now streaked with blood, and spun back to Dolomun, but the shopkeeper had flung the table between them and disappeared through the curtain into the front. Clattering and crashes sounded as he knocked shelves over in his panicked escape.

Khellus sighed as he opened the closet. A man dressed in dark purple and black leather strips slumped to the floor. A velvet mask concealed his features. Khellus didn't bother removing it. A shadesman. A member of the killing mob that worked for the Bloodrose faction within the city - those dedicated to diverting as much profit into their own pockets before they reached the capital.

The slam of a door made him raise his head. His mission might already be compromised, but that didn't mean he needed to let the traitor ruin it further. He ran up the steps and back out into the night air. A few roof hops brought him ahead of the fleeing shopkeeper who took turns at random. Dolomun ran fast for his girth and sedentary occupation. Nevertheless, speed availed him none when Khellus appeared around the next corner and stuck a hard arm out at throat level. Dolomun gagged and clutched at his throat as he toppled. Khellus glanced around; glad to see how the few citizens loitering in the area already scurried away, not wanting any trouble.

As he regained his breath, Dolomun remained on his knees. He now looked worn and haggard, as if the last few minutes had aged him a decade.

"How... how did you know?" he rasped.

Khellus kept one sword drawn, the other in its sheath. This bastard didn't deserve both blades.

"You keep yourself bald so the hair doesn't show the signs," he said. "The twitching caught my eye, though you control it well. The citrus smell is another indicator. Asmoran's got you addicted to *dravillish*, hasn't he? You're on the take. How long?"

The man shuddered. "Three years now. They took me in the middle of the night. Tortured me. Filled me to the brim with the stuff and then let me go, knowing I'd do anything to get more." His eyes brimmed with tears. "Threaten me all you want, but nothing I can say will help you now. Ever since he learned the king had targeted him, he's been avoiding any sort of pattern with his business, his guards, his staff... it all changes from week to week." He babbled as Khellus' grip tightened on the sword hilt. "But I know one thing he doesn't. Let me live and I'll tell you."

Khellus scoffed. "Tell me, and I might let you live."

Dolomun pondered this for a moment before bowing his head. "Groxley is here. Arrived yesterday. My sources say he's been hired to take down Asmoran as well."

Khellus frowned. "Why would that brute be brought in for this sort of work?"

"I don't know. I truly don't."

"But you were going to warn Asmoran."

"Of course I was." Dolomun wept at his feet, enormous tears rolling down his crumpled expression. "You don't understand. What it can drive a man to do. It's this constant hunger, this ever-burning need that consumes everything. It cuts all ties except to the one who supplies satisfaction, however brief." He held up shaking hands. "I can't help myself anymore."

Khellus grimaced. "Then let me help you."

He made the death as swift as possible, though certainly not painless. Dolomun had made his choices and had to pay the consequences.

***

Gnawing on a strip of spiced meat, Khellus studied a corner of Asmoran's estate from down the road. Unlike some of the more sprawling mansions and opulent dwellings, Asmoran had built himself a miniature fortress inside the already inviolable city defences. Khellus's view of the estate was blocked by high walls of red stone, except for the two main

towers. Guards patrolled the parapets at all hours, crossbows and swords at the ready. Three well-defended gates opened occasionally to let tarp-covered wagons enter or exit. Staff came and went through smaller doors set within the gates, under the ever watchful eye of Asmoran's guards.

On the outside, Asmoran appeared to run a thriving spice trade, paving the way for wealthy patrons across the lands to indulge in exotic flavours during banquets and feasts. Plenty of the crates and barrels being carted in and out no doubt held supplies for manufacturing *dravillish*—if not the purified drug itself.

Complicated things, politics and economics, two realms of power that braided together so tightly they were often indistinguishable. It was a poorly kept secret that most of the nobles in Belladain worked with the Bloodroses, taking their cut of various illicit operations. Asmoran's

specialty lay in drug trafficking, and he dominated the trade with ruthless

efficiency. Thanks to him, countless languished in drug dens in most major cities, and innumerable lives were lost to the poisonous brew. Other Belladain nobles invested themselves in gambling operations, brothels, slavery, or other peddling that made Khellus's gut roil in disgust.

At the same time, the kingdom relied on such trade to fill its coffers. Not only would cleansing Belladain of its rotting infrastructure prove enormously costly to the court, but it would also deprive the land of a substantial source of coin. It proved a tricky balancing act to manage such undesirable operations without letting the chaos it invited destroy the kingdom from within.

Asmoran had tipped his personal balance away from the king's favour with openly treasonous talk during several social engagements over the past year. Apparently, his position of power had emboldened him in voicing his true opinions of his liege; rumours spoke of his trying to recruit other nobles to rebellion, with the intent to turn Belladain into its own city-state. Khellus had come to restore the balance and remind the other nobles that while they operated with a certain amount of leeway, limits still existed.

To enforce such limits, though, he needed to figure out how best to penetrate the estate and leave Asmoran a corpse in his wake. The guard patrols had at least two levels of redundancy, so attempting to enter through brute force would be foolish. The walls had been topped with rows of spikes and shattered glass, making climbing a hazardous option. Perhaps he needed to sniff around the sewers to see if any underground channels offered themselves. An unsavoury route, but he'd managed worse before.

Street traffic wound past him as he pondered the alternatives. Few took note of the man lounging in the shade, one more commoner amidst the daily hubbub. However, he took note of them, seeing who came and went from the estate. His surveillance allowed him to spot one man in particular sauntering down the road.

With overly long arms and legs, the man stuck up a head taller than most others. He had short-cropped black hair, with several thin white scars marring his otherwise fair features. A loose yellow tunic made his gut and arms appear baggy, concealing what Khellus knew to be a torso and arms corded with muscle. He munched on a green-and-white vapefruit, making one of his cheeks bulge as he chewed.

Groxley.

The thug passed Khellus without so much as a glance, but the assassin knew the indifference to be a farce. He wouldn't have sauntered down this street except to make a show of it for the sake of his fellow killer. Groxley liked to be seen. He loved to flaunt his work, even while leaving no evidence or witnesses in the aftermath.

Khellus rose and followed ten paces back. Groxley carried no weapons, even to Khellus's trained eye, but he knew from experience how deadly the man's bare hands could be. Groxley stopped and leaned against a hitching post outside a tavern, still noshing his snack. He peered up at Asmoran's estate as well, gawking and grinning like a country yokel stupefied by city life and architecture.

As Khellus came up beside him, Groxley spoke without turning. "'ello, Khellus. Impressive, ain't it? Livin' in a palace like that might make a man feel right near invincible." He looked over and grinned, flashing a gap where an incisor was missing. Khellus remembered knocking the tooth loose during their last meeting. "Good thing we's here to put him in his place, no?"

Khellus joined him in inspecting the walls again. "So, who was foolish enough to hire your witless hide?"

Groxley's grin broadened. "My client prefers to go nameless. Let's just say I'm bein' funded by a father who's lost a coupl'a kids to Asmoran's drug pits. Poor wastrels just couldn't keep away, and now they be feedin' flowers. Daddy don't like that, and wants someone to pay."

"You're here to make Asmoran a spectacle."

"And what's wrong with that?"

"It's messy. Sloppy. A pointless waste of effort."

Groxley spat out a vapefruit seed. "It's fun. Besides, what's it matter? Either way, he's a deader." He bumped Khellus's shoulder with his own. "We're both here for the same job. Why not let me get the grunt work and you get the glory?"

"It's not about glory. You've been hired for nothing but petty revenge."

"You're here for revenge. Just you get to pretend it matters more 'cause it's royal. Only real difference is you ain't being paid."

Khellus scowled. "It's more than money."

Groxley licked the fruit juice off his fingers. "You gotta sad, strange way of seein' life, Khellus."

A subtle gap had formed between them and passers-by, as if the crowd were instinctively clued in to the predators among them and shied away. Khellus stepped closer, in easy reach of the other man's long grasp.

"I know you're too much an idiot to heed any warning to leave."

Groxley gave him a look up and down. "Business, is it? Not personal?"

"There's nothing personal about this."

Picking a fingernail between his teeth, Groxley shrugged. "You sure did take it hard last time, when I got to Lady Ovrida 'afore you."

Khellus kept his face calm, though he seethed inside. "You slaughtered a dozen innocents and left a house in ruins. Only the lady needed to be eliminated."

"What can I say? I'm efficient." Groxley straightened and put a hand on Khellus's shoulder. "You're right. It ain't just about the coin. There's somethin' more."

The assassin met the thug's gaze, unflinching. "What's that?"

"Seein' you're sorry ass slink off after I beat you to the body. Priceless." He tapped his temple with two fingers, a mock salute. "To the better man go the glory."

Khellus sighed as Groxley strolled off and soon became lost in the flow of the street. A complication he didn't need. Gone was the luxury of spending days or weeks in planning. Groxley wouldn't bother with such means. He'd just look for the weakest chink in Asmoran's defences and bull through them until he either reached his target or got dropped trying. Knowing the man's effectiveness, Khellus didn't doubt he'd make a good show of it. If he attacked before Khellus and failed, that'd leave Asmoran locked up even tighter than before, making it near-impossible for the assassin to reach him. If he attacked and succeeded, it'd be a serious undermining of the king's authority and would engender further talk of rebellion.

Khellus needed a swift, sure strike; yet the time constraints grated. Perhaps that's what Groxley intended by showing himself. He wanted to push Khellus into a hasty attempt, hoping he'd trip up and get caught or killed. Maybe he'd even be watching from the side lines, observing to inform his own methods. Even so, every hour counted now.

He fixed eyes back to the estate, trying to pierce its defences, seeking the hole through which he could slip unnoticed. Flaws always existed. It just was a matter of discerning them. Here, the physical obstacles appeared insurmountable. Perhaps he could bribe a guard, though, or sneak in on one of the supply deliveries.

After another hour of observation, he discarded those ideas. The wagons in and out were too well-inspected, and it'd take too long to figure out the traffic patterns, isolate a wagon, and build a false compartment to conceal himself. The guards would also be a tricky approach, requiring careful study to single out a possible patsy, and if he guessed wrong and his target refused, he'd have to kill the man or keep him locked and bound somewhere; and the estate would be put on alert anyways once the guard went missing.

Not only that, but he picked out signs of *dravillish* usage among the guards as well as a number of visitors. Little mystery then as to how Asmoran ensured the loyalty of key people within his operation. As Dolomun had proven, such individuals would betray country and king to secure a steady supply, whether they truly wanted to or not.

More complications.

He stilled as two figures in the crowd caught his eyes. A young woman held a girl's hand as they wove through the crowd. The woman's brown hair had been done up in a neat bun and she wore a simple dress of blue trimmed with golden lace. The girl skipped alongside her, tugging at her mother's hand. She had indigo-black hair down to her shoulders, and a red dress clad her skinny frame.

Though it had been six years, Khellus recognized Abrodail the instant he spotted her. Her lithe gait remained the same, reminding him of how she'd first caught his gaze with the way she almost danced among the tavern tables and patrons as she delivered food and drink. When she pulled the girl out of the way of an oncoming cart, Khellus glimpsed the same curve of her lips, the familiar dip of her collarbone. He wondered if her hair smelled the same.

Shaking off the nostalgia, he glanced at the girl again. A child? A father? Married then. He smiled to himself. Good for her. From their clothes, they looked to be well-cared for, and their easy manner suggested contentment with their lot. Well, whatever happened during his mission, this glimpse of the past had at least given him a scrap of hope for…

His smile faded as the pair aimed for one of the estate gates. A guard intercepted them, spoke with Abrodail briefly, and then opened one of the smaller doors to admit them. When the door shut and cut off Khellus's view, he remained staring for a few minutes. Options tumbled through his mind.

She didn't come with any other deliveries, nor did she bear paperwork or materials of any sort, so it was unlikely that she represented an outside business, especially with a child in tow. Asmoran remained a staunch bachelor, though he had his pick of noble decadents who flocked about him anytime he appeared in public. Could she be a consort of some sort? Khellus tossed this thought aside as quick as it came. Asmoran wouldn't entangle himself with anyone lower than his station. The guards obviously knew her, so she came to the estate on a regular basis. She must work there as part of Asmoran's staff.

Now his lips pinched in a thin line, a determined grimace.

There. There was his in.

Chapter 2

That evening, as the sky dimmed and the city brightened, the pair re-emerged. Abrodail's hair now hung in a loosened braid, while the child pranced along as energetically as ever. Khellus held back in the shadows as they passed, and then slipped into their footsteps. They walked without fear through the dwindling foot traffic until, half an hour later, they reached a more domestic stretch of city blocks. There, small homes nestled side by side, replacing shopfronts with cosier abodes, where candles, lanterns, and faelights flickered in the windows. Children darted about, but Abrodail's daughter didn't join them. Instead, she watched the play with a distant curiosity, as if uncertain what these other laughing, scampering creatures might be.

At last, they reached one home with a clay-tiled roof and a green door. Abrodail and the child went inside, leaving Khellus to ponder his next move from across the street. Her husband didn't appear home, so he'd need to time this well. The fewer involved, the better.

Choosing the straightforward approach, he strode up to the door and knocked. After a moment, footsteps pattered up. The latch clicked and the door opened a few inches, enough to let one of the girl's dark eyes peer up at him.

"Hello," she said in the serious manner of a child. "Who are you?"

He tried for a harmless smile. "Hello. I'm an old friend of your mothers."

Her face scrunched up. "No you aren't."

Khellus raised an eyebrow. "Why do you say that?"

"'Cause mommy's friends are all nice, and you don't look nice."

He crouched, arms on his knees. She didn't draw back, though she remained clinging to the latch. "Sometimes," he said, "nice-looking people aren't, and people who don't look nice are. And sometimes there need to be not-nice people to do not-nice jobs. Don't you think?"

She swung the door wider in order to confront him with crossed arms. "Is that s'posed to be a puzzle?"

"Does it confuse you?"

"No. You just make it sound c'fusing."

Khellus chuckled. "Maybe I'm trying to confuse you."

"That's not nice."

"Eogwen," Abrodail called, rushing into view. "What've I told you about answering the—oh gods above and below." She halted for a second, colour leeching from her cheeks. After a second, she hurried forward and pulled Eogwen back, pushing her off down the hall. "Little flower, go read until your father gets home."

Khellus rose as the girl skip off. "She can read. That's good. I was at least twice her age before I learned how."

Abrodail stared at him, hand on the door as if debating whether to slam it or not. Then she swallowed and firmed her shoulders. "You shouldn't be here."

"Probably not. Nevertheless..." Khellus spread his hands.

Various expressions cast shadows over her face, like clouds over the sun. "You're not here for me."

"I wasn't at first. I initially came on business."

Her laughter still sent a tiny thrill through him, even laced with scorn as it was. "A job. I should've known."

"Yes, you should have."

"What do you want? You're obviously not dropping in to comment on my daughter's schooling, so that means I've something to do with whatever business you're about."

"Can I come in?"

"No."

They engaged in a silent stand-off until Khellus gave way. "Wescel Asmoran. He's your employer, isn't he?"

"Oh, devils take you, you utter bastard." She moved to slam the door, but he jammed a boot and shoulder in the gap. Abrodail struggled to dislodge him, to no avail. "Get away from us. I want nothing to do with you."

"Just hear me out, Abby, would you?"

"Don't call me that."

"Rah!" Something struck Khellus' boot over and over. He and Abrodail looked down at Eogwen, who had thrown herself between her mother's legs and now stabbed at Khellus' toes with a wooden fork. "Go away!"

Khellus cleared his throat as Abrodail swept her daughter up and hustled her back into the house. She returned half a minute later, looking flustered. This turned to a glare. "You're still here."

"I'd appreciate it if you let me at least explain."

She raised a finger. "One word. You get one word."

"Treason." She froze. Khellus pushed the door a little wider. "Abrodail, your employer is a traitor to the king and he's at the head of a growing faction working to undermine the safety of this entire region. I can't believe that someone as smart as you could work there without picking up on that." He leaned in until he caught her eye, though she still refused to look at him straight on. "You know it's true."

"What if it is?" she asked. "I'm just a clerk. A minor one, at that."

"Perhaps. But if Asmoran is left alone too long, he'll likely succeed and rile up much if not all of the city to open rebellion. It's just a matter of time. You know what unchecked treason leads to, don't you? War." He tilted his head at the rest of the house, indicating her now-absent daughter. "You want to raise a child in a city under siege?"

She slumped ever so slightly. "Shades take me, I forgot how convincing you could be. I shouldn't have given you a single word." She sighed and stepped aside. "Get in here before someone sees you."

He slid into the front hall. She latched the door behind him and then led him into a receiving room. While not luxurious by any stretch, it held several cushioned chairs, a small table, and light decorations of potted flowers and cheap art fixtures. A flight of stone and wood stairs led to a second story, where he guessed the bedrooms were. Eogwen sat almost hidden over in a corner nook, legs tucked up as she paged through a slim book. She gave the appearance of studiousness, but Khellus kept catching her glancing at him. After the third time, she stuck her tongue out and slumped so the book hid her face.

He tugged his gloves off as he took a chair by the ashen hearth. Abrodail took up the chair furthest from him. Her lips twitched in the manner that told him she restrained herself from unleashing a torrent of words. Scathing ones, no doubt. Funny how a few months with a person could leave their smallest mannerisms engrained in the memory. Odder yet how much the years could leave one unchanged.

Glancing around, he pretended to not have already scrutinized the layout. "Cosy."

She poured water from a pitcher into a polished ebonwood mug, pointedly not offering him any. "We're happy here."

"Are you?"

"Yes. Favriel is a good man and Eogwen makes every day a delight. I don't want you disrupting our lives. So say what you have to and then be gone before he gets home."

"If all goes well, I'll be gone in a day and I'll have averted far bigger disruptions in the process."

She gave a delicate snort. "How often do things go well around you, Khellus?"

"We aren't allowed many mistakes in my line of work."

Abrodail's gaze lingered on Eogwen, who hummed as she flipped through her little book. At last, she roused and took a deep breath. "So. Asmoran." She pitched her voice low, so the child wouldn't overhear.

"Yes."

"You're here to kill him."

"Yes."

"And for some reason, you need my help. I don't see what I can offer, unless you're looking for a place to hide. We've got a root cellar with a few empty barrels you can tuck inside."

Khellus smirked. "A gracious offer, but I'll pass. No, what I need is simple. Getting inside."

She licked her lips. "They're comfortable barrels."

He leaned forward. "I'm serious. Time is essential in this, and I need to be inside the estate grounds by tomorrow morning, if possible."

A trapped look entered her brown eyes. He'd seen it before, most often right before he plunged a blade through a target's heart. "Six years, Khellus."

For the first time, he dropped his gaze. "Did it mean so much to you?"

"Didn't it to you?"

He sat back. "You knew I'd have to leave. Where my duty lay."

"Perhaps. We often fool ourselves far more than we realize. Even so, I didn't think your duty would involve slipping away in the middle of the night without so much as a goodbye."

"I left a note."

"I burned it."

He suppressed a wince. "Can we go back to talking about business?"

"You mean talking about killing the nobleman who lets us remain..." She waved at the home in general. "Cosy?"

"You've every right to be angry, but please don't let that stop you from doing the right thing. If it helps, don't think of me as that man anymore."

"I don't think of you as much of a man at all."

Devils below, she'd sharpened over the years. He took a few seconds to corral his thoughts. While he'd expected a lashing of this sort, he didn't fully understand where her cold fury came from. She practically

radiated with it. Yes, he'd abandoned her, he admitted it. Unfair to her, but she seemed to have done well since, despite everything. He'd been drawn to her inner strength, her passion, when they first crossed paths but that

passion had been tempered since he saw her last. Turned a bit more to steel.

He tried again. "What I mean is, don't let your bitterness against me, for the way I wronged you, sway you into denying me outright. Don't see me as Khellus, but as a hand of the king. Someone who is trying to save a good number of lives."

Abrodail sipped from her water. "By taking lives."

"A life. One that is malicious and corrupt and is poisoning all those around him."

She looked away. "You don't realize what that would do to us."

Something in her voice snagged his attention. "What do you mean?"

As she hesitated, footsteps thumped overhead. Khellus came to his feet, a hand going to a sword hilt. "I thought you were waiting for your husband to get home?"

Abrodail's eyes widened. Apparently she hadn't heard anything. "I am. He always comes home after us."

"Daddy's upstairs," Eogwen said. "He was here sleeping when we got home."

Abrodail rose as well. "Why didn't you say anything?"

Eogwen shrugged and went back to reading.

A man's voice called down. "Abby? Is that you?"

Khellus caught Abrodail's eye and mouthed, *Abby?*

Shut up, she mouthed back. "A moment, darling." She grabbed Khellus' arm and steered him for the front. Before they got two steps, a man appeared at the top of the stairs and tromped down. Slim and trim, he had a shock of thick, blond hair and sharp features that gave him a vulpine look. His blue-and-crimson uniform appeared rumpled from being slept in, the only unkempt thing about him.

"Hope I didn't startle, dove, I simply—" He paused in mid-step and grabbed the wooden railing to steady himself. "Who's this?"

Khellus noted how his hand reached for a non-existent weapon at his waist. So, a man unafraid to defend his household. Admirable.

"Mommy's not-nice friend," Eogwen said.

"Hush, little flower." Abrodail released Khellus's arm and stepped back a pace. "Favriel, this is...yes, he's a friend. An old friend I haven't seen in a long time. His name is..."

"Khellus." Khellus stepped over and offered a hand.

Favriel eyed him askance as he briefly accepted the clasp. A light floral scent surrounded the man, reminiscent of freshly watered roses. "Oh? I've a mind for faces and names, but I fear yours isn't coming to it. I assume we've not crossed paths before."

"I'm not from Belladain," Khellus said. "Just here on business."

The other man's gaze flicked from him to Abrodail. "And past visits have involved my wife?"

"It's been years since our last meeting. Before you were together, I'd wager. I hope you don't take this as any sort of impropriety."

Awareness flared in the Favriel's eyes. "Shades take me." He peered closer at Khellus. "This is him, isn't it?"

"Oh, trample me now." Abrodail massaged her forehead. "I'm not ready for this."

Khellus looked between them. "You told him about me? I'm touched."

Favriel laughed mirthlessly. "Not of you, specifically. But when we married, I had cause to know of your existence."

"Did you? "Khellus frowned. "When did you marry?"

"We exchanged oaths three years ago."

"And she still spoke of me?"

It was Abrodail's turn to laugh. "You can be quite the dunce, Khellus. Listen." She took his shoulders, forcing him to turn so the three of them formed a triangle. "Eogwen is my daughter, but not Favriel's."

Cold prickles rippled down Khellus from crown to toes.

"She's yours."

"You're sure?" Khellus asked.

Abrodail huffed. "That's the fourth time you asked. The answer's not changing and if you ask again, it'll get you slapped. With a brick."

The three of them sat around the table, Khellus on one side, the couple on the other. Eogwen had been sent to rummage up a treat for herself in the pantry, and she occasionally darted out with selection which she offered up for approval—an entire wheel of cheese, a wine flask, a box of pepper. With each rejected item, she slunk back to scrounge up another option.

Khellus watched her go with her latest choice, a salted slab of mutton. "I suppose she's the right age. But why didn't you—"

"Why didn't I what?" Abrodail made a fist. "Write to let you know? Chase after you? You made your feelings rather clear by leaving, and if I gave up everything here to track you down in the hopes of some paternal fondness, it'd mean surrendering what little life I'd managed to build here." She sighed deeply. "Besides, I didn't want her to have a father who might never be around. Knowing your sort of business, I figured you'd forever be traveling, off on one mission or another until you got killed."

He drummed fingers on the table. "Fair enough." To be honest, he felt relief at never having being dragged into Eogwen's upbringing. It would've been one more complication, one more chain wrapped around his soul. Personal attachments of that sort always muddled the mind and heart, liabilities an assassin couldn't afford. He looked to Favriel, who wore a bemused expression. "I'll admit, you're taking this rather calmly."

Favriel shrugged. "I came to terms with it when I married Abby. I love Eogwen like my own and would do anything to see she comes to no harm." His voice and face hardened.

Khellus held up a hand. "I'm not here with any intent to take her from you."

The man relaxed, if barely. "Then why are you here? I'll assume it's no social calling."

Khellus eyed his uniform. "You work for Asmoran as well?"

Favriel drew shoulders back. "Indeed. I'm one of his chief stewards."

"Must be nice, both of you working there."

The other man smiled. "It has its advantages. We've no need to leave Eogwen with a marm. We get meals together and catch little times alone, so long as it doesn't interfere with our work. Many staff have family members who serve minor functions throughout the operations. It gives the whole affair a rather close feel."

Khellus quelled a grimace. A great way for Asmoran to maintain an eye on his staff at large, recruit new addicts, and have plenty of blackmail opportunities to keep any potential dissenters in line. Abrodail looked tense as she watched Favriel and averted her eyes when Khellus tried to meet them.

"You want help from me, you tell him as well. He's loved me, cared for me and for Eogwen, and he's never abandoned us and never will. He deserves to know."

Acquiescing, Khellus kept it as brief as possible. He used the same arguments he had to get in the door with Abrodail. Asmoran. The king's edict. The talk of rebellion and the need to make an example to keep the other nobles in line before war broke out and threatened the whole region—their family included.

To his credit, Favriel maintained his poise throughout the explanation, the only sign of tension being the occasional clenching of his jaw. When Khellus finished, Favriel sagged, as if a knot had loosened in his back.

"I see." He scratched at the light stubble on his chin. "This is... vexing."

He stared at his lap for a full minute, while Khellus and Abrodail watched each other over the table. For once, he couldn't read her expression.

At last, Favriel regained his composure. "I'm afraid I can't help you. Neither of us can. You need to leave. Now."

Abrodail laid a hand on his forearm. "Darling-"

Favriel cut her off with an open palm. "I'm sorry, dove. As much as it pains me, I can tell a small part of you still cares for this man despite all the trouble he's caused you. As I said before, I won't see Eogwen or you come to any harm. No matter what the cost."

Khellus stood and planted fists on the table. "You don't see what's at stake here?"

Favriel smirked up at him. "Actually, I do. More than you know. You don't think I'm aware of my lord's dark dealings? The whole city knows it. The whole kingdom, apparently, considering your presence here. However, for us, Lord Asmoran is a boon. He has never been anything but kind and generous to his staff, and it is by his graces that we are able to live in relative comfort and safety." His expression gained a weary edge. "I've gone to great lengths to ensure both Abby and I are involved in the mundane side of his business in rather essential ways. We're safe so long as the status quo is maintained. You remove Asmoran and you doom us and everyone under him. When a noble house falls, none who belong to it are spared. You know this. Servants are captured and tortured for information. Extended family are killed in their beds."

"Worse will happen when armies march on Belladain."

"You're so certain it'll come to that," said Favriel. "What if you're wrong?"

"Whether I am or not, I act under orders from the king. The same king Asmoran is supposed to serve as you, by proxy, are to do as well."

Favriel splayed his hands. "Will the king come here and give us new jobs? Pay us monthly wages? See our families fed?"

Khellus sighed through his nose. While Abrodail had seemed willing to listen to him earlier, the more her husband spoke, the more he sensed her withdrawing. He stalked around the table and they turned their chairs until he stood before them like a supplicant at the feet of royalty.

"You're with him on this?" he asked Abrodail.

Her cheeks quirked with unspoken words for a few seconds before she grasped her husband's hand. "I'm sorry, Khellus. If it were me alone, perhaps. This is too much."

He nodded and tucked thumbs into his belt. "I see. Then I'm sorry for what I have to do next."

Their quizzical expressions turned to shock as he snapped one hand out. Even as Favriel tried to rise, Khellus jabbed a black thorn into the meat of his throat. The man's eyes bugged as he fell back, slumped and motionless in his chair.

Abrodail rose with a cry. "What've you done?"

"Expedited my mission." He held up the thorn. "This is plucked from the *fava-drul* plant, a rather noxious growth from South Byabara. It's a slow-acting poison that will leave him permanently crippled within a day and will prove lethal within two. I have the antidote, but will only provide it after you've helped me enter the estate—and once I've seen Asmoran dead. Getting me in and warning the guards after won't do any good."

Abrodail gaped in horror, and Khellus clamped down on the squirm of guilt in his gut. He'd have preferred to use the *fava-drul* thorn to incapacitate a guard or errant servant. Contrary to what he'd said, it paralyzed but didn't kill. Favriel would be perfectly fine within a day, and the deception would hopefully spur Abrodail to necessary action.

A crash snapped their attention to the kitchen threshold, where Eogwen had dropped a clay jug of cream. "Daddy!" She splattered a milky puddle underfoot as she raced to Favriel. She must've cut her sole on a shard, for a trickle of blood turned her footprints pink.

Eogwen tugged at Favriel's limp arm until Abrodail pulled her away. Abrodail hugged her weeping child... Khellus' child... and tried to hush her, assuring her everything would be all right. Daddy was just very tired and needed another nap. She bustled the girl upstairs, and soft sobs continued to float down until they trailed off. Khellus loitered, assuming that Eogwen had cried herself to sleep.

Trying to be helpful, he dragged Favriel out of the chair and laid him on the floor, positioned so the man wouldn't wake with a horrid crick in his neck. He straightened just as Abrodail reappeared on the stairs. She came down halfway and stopped to gaze at him in aghast wonder.

"You really aren't him anymore, are you?"

Khellus stepped away from her husband, hands clasped behind his back. "No. Have you made your decision?"

Her hand tightened on the rail. "Devils damn you for this, Khellus."

"I'll accept that if necessary. Abby—" He paused at her murderous look and corrected. "Abrodail, there's another killer out there already targeting your lord, a monster even worse than I am."

"Hard to believe."

"Compared to him, I'm a kindly butcher that puts down a fatted calf in a single blow. He'll slaughter the whole herd just to reach the calf, slit its belly open, and choke it to death on its own organs. The reality is Asmoran is going to die no matter what. Best it be by my hand and by royal command rather than by a brute who'll leave the city in chaos. Believe it or not, I'm trying to protect you."

"By poisoning my husband and terrorising your own daughter?"

"The former is a necessity. The latter would only matter if she knew and if I cared. As you yourself said, someone like me should never be responsible for an innocent flower like herself."

Abrodail came the rest of the way down to stand at arm's length from him. Favriel lay between them, breathing steady. Her hand shook ever so slightly as she pointed at Khellus.

"I want you to swear not on your honour, because you obviously have none but on the very bond you have to the king. Swear that once you're done here, you'll leave and we'll never see you again. Ever. Not a glimpse, not a whisper."

He made a shallow bow. "Done. Shall we get to it then?"

She blinked. "Right now?"

He nodded at her husband. "You'd rather wait until tomorrow, when permanent damage might've already set in?"

"Bastard." She gritted teeth. "Fine. How do we go about this?"

Chapter 3

Harsh magelights floated over the guards' heads as they kept their posts outside the gate. Whilst the conjured lights illuminated a patch of the road, Khellus knew it would also spoil their night vision. He counted on this fact as he observed the gate from not more than ten paces away. While now wearing one of Favriel's blue-and-crimson coats over his tunic, the simple disguise wouldn't be any help if he just marched up and asked to be admitted. The guards would be overly alert for any faces they didn't recognise. Instead, he'd appropriated it more for avoiding too much scrutiny once within the walls, though the swords hidden beneath his cloak might still draw attention if he dawdled.

For now, Khellus remained concealed in a swathe of shadows cast by a clump of thick vines snaking up the estate wall. It didn't reach more than halfway up the wall, and so hadn't been chopped down as a possible climbing hazard, but it provided enough cover for someone who knew how to blend in. The earlier crowds had thinned as people ducked into their homes for dinner, or taverns for drink. By the time

Khellus had arranged the plan with Abrodail and gotten into position, the emerald moon hung heavy overhead.

The guards held muttered conversation as he waited, and he caught snatches of gossip and complaints about loitering beggars. One guard drew out a tiny wooden box and dabbed a finger into the contents before wiping this inside his nostrils. After this, all signs of fatigue fled as his posture straightened and his eyes glistened a bit brighter. More *dravillish*,. Khellus wondered if Asmoran used it himself, but figured the man overseeing such a large operation would be smart enough to avoid becoming addicted to the very substance he trafficked.

A quarter candle later, Abrodail appeared down the street, coming from the same direction as she had that morning. She wore her earlier dress, identifying her as one of Asmoran's servants. She'd left Eogwen locked in at home with a stern command to keep watch over her daddy.

The guards perked up at her approach, though they looked more confused than concerned. For her part, Abrodail maintained her poise well enough. If she felt any strain from being forced into this arrangement, it didn't show beyond the stiffness of her shoulders and neck—easily attributed to fatigue from a day's work. Khellus reached into a pouch and drew out a slender crystal as long as his thumb. He held it between the forefingers and thumbs of both hands, waiting for the right moment.

One of the guards met her at the gate while the other remained back by the servant door.

"Business so late?" he asked.

Abrodail smile wearily. "Business never ends. My husband is working on an urgent shipment for the end of the week and wanted to double-check several orders. But he left his ledger in the office and sent me to retrieve it."

The guard bowed slightly and nodded at the other, who drew out a latchkey and opened the inner door. Right as he swung it wide to admit Abrodail, Khellus shut his eyes and snapped the crystal between his fingers.

The nullification spell contained within the crystal activated and the gate's magelights winked out. Plunged into darkness, the guards shouted and stomped about. Khellus opened his eyes, still able to see perfectly, and dashed for the door. One guard had Abrodail by the arm while the other had drawn his sword and stared blindly out at the street.

Khellus slipped by them, unseen, and into the court beyond. Nobody stood in sight. Marble columns supported a covered walkway to his right while empty stables occupied the left side, and several doors ringed the wide court. According to Abrodail, this gate protected the main staffing section of the estate, leading into larger storage areas, a kitchen, and workrooms. The estate proper thrust up in front of him, a stately affair of four main towers forming the corners of the enormous manor.

Taking this all in at a glance, he ducked behind a marble column. A second later, the spell ended and the magelights flared back into being, further disrupting the guards' sight. Once they settled, they held a hurried conversation before admitting Abrodail and slamming the door shut behind her. No doubt they'd be adding fickle conjurers to their list of nightly complaints. Khellus tapped a breast pocket, making sure his second crystal remained in place. This one held an enchantment that would protect him from any scryers or divinations, as

Abrodail had assured him Asmoran had several skilled mages in his service.

Abrodail waited until Khellus's soft whistle drew her over. She scowled as she joined him beside the column.

"What now?"

He cocked his head at the main building. "You know where Asmoran takes dinner and sleeps?"

"Oh, yes, of course. I often bring him a mug of warm muckmilk and tuck him in at night." She sighed. "I have a general idea, but I don't frequent that part of the estate often."

He nudged her into motion. "Best guide I've got for now. Let's keep moving."

They eased out of the shadows. Dozens of windows lined the estate's stone walls, many lit from within by faelights, magelights, and hanging lamps. No smoking torches here to spoil the appearance of a refined manor.

Abrodail led the way a few steps ahead, Khellus using her slight frame to block immediate views of himself. Entering the nearest door deposited them in a long corridor lined by a variety of storerooms. They passed pantries lined with dried herbs and fresh produce, as well as sacks of grain, rice, and beans. Abrodail noted one stairwell leading down into a wine cellar, and another to the cheese and meat larder. They paused outside the entrance to the main kitchen as Khellus pondered the most expedient approach.

Even at such a late hour, staff and servants bustled around, though none gave the pair any regard as they hurried from task to task. In the kitchen, pots boiled and the smell of cooking meat laced the air. Khellus noted only one cook at work, toiling over large clumps of floury dough. When the man's back was turned, Khellus darted in and snatched up a small meat pie sitting on a counter.

Abrodail looked at him in silent confusion when he rejoined her. He shrugged as he polished off the pie in a few bites.

"What? I'm hungry and you didn't offer dinner." Ignoring the roll of her eyes, he pointed along the hall. "Where's Favriel's office?"

She guided him down several more halls and up two flights of stairs. He held her back at one juncture when footsteps alerted him, and they remained tucked around a corner until the sound faded into nothing. At last, climbing several more flights, she entered a dark room where a low fire waged a losing battle against the shadows.

Taking down a poker, she stoked the flames brighter to reveal a long, low chamber full of desks and bookshelves. Halfway down, a pair of smoke-glass doors led out onto a small balcony.

"This is where Favriel and the other stewards convene during the day," she said, staring into the fire. "We shouldn't be disturbed."

Khellus paced the length of the chamber and back, ensuring no steward had decided to sleep over in one of the corners or under a desk. Scrolls and tomes of all sizes and ages lined the shelves in orderly bundles and stacks, and a sharp odour of fresh ink tickled his nose.

He opened the balcony doors and gazed out. The balcony faced inward over the estate, giving him a clear view of the other three towers, several other courtyards, a lushly tended garden, and small training yard populated by wood and straw fighting dummies. The estate roof sat at near a ten foot drop below the balcony, spotted with patches of broken tile and the occasional fireplace chimney. Sections slanted up against one another, forming a clay and stone patchwork of grimy red and white.

Abrodail came alongside him and pointed out one tower in particular. "When not entertaining guests, Lord Asmoran spends most of his evenings in the north western tower. The main dining hall is located at its base and I believe his sleeping suite is a few flights above this."

Khellus eyed the tower, inspecting each window and balcony across the way in case Asmoran decided to pick that moment to appear at one of them. No such fortune, however. He'd have to creep across the manor grounds, hoping to avoid any guard patrols and overly alert staff, and then search the tower room-by-room until he found the one Asmoran occupied. Such an effort would take all night, leaving far too much margin for error or unforeseen circumstances to ruin the attempt.

Unless... "Stay here until I return."

So saying, he strode over and hopped up onto the balcony railing. Abrodail gasped as he dropped over the edge. However, he turned as he fell and caught himself on the lip of the balcony, feet braced against the stones below. After another measured pause, he let go and fell to the roof.

Tiles cracked underfoot as he landed. He rolled through the landing, bruising his back and sides against the hard edges. As his momentum stalled, he remained lying flat in case any guards along the walls looked for the source of the brief clatter.

On his back, he caught sight of Abrodail staring down at him in wonder. Then, with a shake of her head, she ducked back inside the room and shut the doors. Hopefully she'd continue to hold her husband's life in higher regard than her lord's and stay still and silent until he finished the task.

After slowing his breaths and making sure no alarm rose, he pushed up into a crouch and surveyed the area. The main stretch of the northern wall was visible from this vantage point, which meant any on it might see him in return. He shuffled behind a stone chimney and peered out from around it until he got his bearings. Moving from chimney to abutment to chimney, he made his way across the roof, careful not to dislodge further tiles and send any crashing to the courtyards below.

When he reached the north western tower, Khellus crept along the curving wall until he spotted another balcony some fifteen feet above. While the tower had been mastercrafted, no doubt, time had weathered it, leaving plenty of chinks and gaps in the stone. Using these, Khellus wove his way back up. He prayed the guards would be fixed on the possibility of external threats and not turn their gazes inward at an inopportune moment.

He reached the balcony and latched onto the railing. Easing upwards, he peered over the edge. Through the smoke-glass doors, the room beyond appeared empty. He swung a leg up and over, and then gained his footing to stand firm.

The room — simple quarters with a bed, armoire, and wash basin — did indeed remain dark and void of any threats. He went to the door and opened it slightly to peek out. A dim hall curved away in both directions. Nobody in sight, though the occasional tapestry and painted portrait added a splash of colour to the muted decor. After waiting and listening for a couple minutes, Khellus emerged and followed the hall until it came to stairs going both up and down.

As he debated which way, voices floated down from the upper landing. He retreated into an alcove inhabited by a life-sized statue of a soldier in full battle regalia. From this hiding spot, he listened as two people made their way past.

"Don't understand it," came a woman's voice. "Sometimes the master is ravenous enough to gnaw a gruckbelly to gristle. Other times he don't eat for what seems like weeks. Where's he pack it away?"

"Hush," said a man. "Don't be speaking ill of Lord Asmoran. Every noble's odd in their own way, and if his diet's the strangest thing we've to manage, we're on the good side of fate to serve him. Take the platter down to the hall and leave it to cool. If the master changes his mind, he'll go down to eat when he's right and ready."

Their voices and footsteps faded, and a scent of roasted duck lingered in their wake. Khellus came out from behind the statue and headed up the stairs. Three flights higher, and he came out on a level with plush carpets and warmer lights burning along the walls. Marble busts sat on pedestals that lined the main hall up to a massive set of oak double-doors.

The lack of guards surprised Khellus, but he supposed guards would've been posted at lower entrances and stairways, with no one expecting a person to enter via a balcony halfway up the tower.

He paced over and lifted a latch. The door swung on oiled hinges, and he pushed it open just wide enough to sidle inside, and then let it softly click shut again. He stood in a well-lit sitting room with richly embroidered chairs, settees, and side tables. Sculptures and paintings crowded the walls, interspersed with antiquated armour fixtures. Three darkened thresholds all led off from this first room, and Khellus inspected the closest first. It held a bedroom, with an enormous canopied feather bed. No one slept in it, as of yet. The next contained an opulent washroom, complete with an entire wall made of mirrors.

As he approached the third, Khellus drew his swords. A scritching noise caught his ear as he neared. Entering this room, he noted two more doors set in opposing walls. However, his attention quickly locked on the man at the far end of the room.

Wescel Asmoran sat at an ornate redwood desk, writing on parchment by the light of a lone candle. He paused to sip from a goblet of wine and then resumed his notations.

Candlelight made his brown hair look bronze and accentuated the deep folds of his silk robe. While he'd made his fortune as a soldier, Asmoran had lost his trim figure to the trappings of nobility, adding jowls to his cheeks and a pendulous weight to his gut. A balding spot peeked through otherwise thick hair, though Khellus didn't discern any of the yellow streaks indicative of *dravillish* use — as he'd guessed.

Khellus closed the gap one silent footfall at a time. Right as he neared the halfway point of the room, Asmoran laid down his quill and slugged back the rest of his wine. Then the noble turned and smiled at the assassin.

"You took your time," he said.

The doors on either side burst open and a dozen guards sprinted into the room. Half aimed crossbows at Khellus while the rest wielded bared blades. It happened in half a heartbeat. A well-planned trap.

Far outnumbered, Khellus slowly lowered his swords to the floor. The instant he rose from doing so, four guards grabbed hold of him and shoved him to his knees. One wrenched his arms behind his back while the other laid a sharp edge against his throat.

A pair of guards went around the room and lit numerous lamp fixtures until all shadows had been chased away. Asmoran pushed up from his chair, jowls quivering. He scratched the side of his crooked nose as he strode over to inspect his would-be killer. His voice had a scratchy edge to it, much like the quill he'd just been writing with.

"So, this is the hidden blade the king sends in an attempt to spill my blood." He sneered down at Khellus as if he'd accidentally stepped in a dung pile. "I wonder what his response will be when I send him your head back instead."

"The king cares nothing for me," Khellus said. "I'm just one servant. He'll send another."

"I'm sure. However, this is exactly the sort of impetus I need to completely rally the other lords behind me. Once they see how desperate and fearful the king is, they'll be emboldened to finally take action. A few pathetic assassination attempts will only further our resolve."

Khellus gazed at the hard-eyed guards surrounding him. They'd been in place. Ready. Waiting. "How did you know? Or do you always have a few squads in your quarters to keep you company?"

Asmoran chuckled. "I've had you tracked ever since you crossed inside my walls. My mages alerted me the moment you set foot here and have monitored your progress the whole way." He smirked at Khellus's puzzled looked. "You thought yourself warded against such measures, didn't you? Well, never fear. Your charms worked well enough. My mages couldn't see you directly. However, if one knows that an assassin is about, one concealed by magical means, scryers can still detect the spell in effect, blocking them from seeing clearly. It's like tracking a bird in the sky by the shadow it casts upon the ground."

"That means somebody warned you," Khellus said. "Who?"

Asmoran clasped hands over his belly. "My operation thrives on the undying loyalty of my servants." He waved at one of the side rooms the guards had hidden in. "Come on out. It's perfectly safe now."

Favriel stepped into sight, Eogwen at his side. She clutched one of his hands while holding her wooden fork in the other. For once, Khellus found himself dumbfounded.

"How..." The *fava-drul* thorn should've kept Favriel insensate until the following evening at least.

"I gave daddy his medicine," Eogwen said. "It woke him up."

Favriel grimaced. "Our little flower is a resourceful one, even if she doesn't exactly understand what she's attempting to do."

"I do too," Eogwen cried. "You use medicine all'a time. I gave you more."

"*Dravillish*," Khellus said flatly. "You lied about not being involved in the drug operations." The man's blond hair hid that sign well enough and the floral perfume he wore concealed the citrus scent of a habitual user.

Favriel flushed. "About myself, perhaps. Abrodail and our little flower remain innocent, though, and I sacrifice myself to keep them that way. I'll do anything to make sure we're cared for. That includes stopping you from destroying our master. Once I woke, I caught a carriage here straightaway and managed to arrive just a bit ahead of you."

Khellus sighed. "Favriel, you utter fool. You don't realize what you've done here, do you?"

The other man frowned and made to speak, but cut off as guards escorted Abrodail into the room. She looked confounded at the scene, but then her confusion melted into relief at seeing Favriel and Eogwen. Her husband rushed to embrace her while Eogwan tried to cling to both their legs. Abrodail crouched to kiss her daughter's forehead, and then rose, hand-in-hand with Favriel.

"What's happened?" she asked. Then she focused on Asmoran and curtsied. "M'lord? It's good to see you safe."

He smiled softly.

"Eogwen got into your husband's *dravillish* stash," Khellus said. "She dosed him, thinking it was medicine and woke him up from the stupor." He met her astounded gaze. "It was never lethal, Abby. I lied to trick you into helping me."

"*Dravillish?*" Abrodail turned to Favriel, who wouldn't meet her eye. "But you said... "

"Heartbreaking to see each of us deceived in our way," said Asmoran. He gestured to one group of guards. "Take them. Bring the girl to me."

Abrodail and Favriel were too shocked to struggle as guards clamped down on them with merciless hands. Eogwen wailed as another guard dragged her over to Asmoran's side.

Favriel jerked against those holding him. "Wait. Lord Asmoran. What is this?"

The noble's expression dipped into a mournful look. "I am so terribly sorry you became involved in this. You've truly been one of the best stewards to ever serve under me." He nodded to the guards. "Kill them as swiftly and painlessly as possible."

The terror on Eogwen's face wrenched something inside Khellus. "No," he shouted. "They're not responsible for any of this. I forced them into it. Spare them, whatever you do to me."

"An assassin begging mercy for others?" Asmoran boggled in mock amazement. "Surely we live in an age of wonders. However, I fear I cannot comply. Given the sensitive nature of my business, I must have staff I can trust implicitly to protect my investments, even at the cost of their own lives." He bowed to Abrodail. "Whether you wished to or not, you have betrayed this estate." He turned to Favriel. "At the same time, I can hardly execute her for treachery and expect you to remain loyal, can I?"

"M'lord, we... I warned you of the assassin! We've given our lives to you."

"So you did and so you shall. I will reward you by not putting your daughter to death along with you. She'll come into my care for the time being. Your little flower, you call her? Charming. I'll see she's... well-tended."

The glint in the noble's eyes told Khellus all he needed to know about the man's intentions. He envisioned Eogwen as a young woman, dull-eyed and drooling as an elderly Asmoran pawed at her, a plaything for nobility, her mind and body enslaved and ruined by years of abuse.

No. Devils damn him. He'd not allow it. No child should suffer so because of him. Not at any cost. He just didn't know how he could live up to this silent oath.

No opportunity offered itself as the guards moved to obey their lord. Abrodail and Favriel wept and cursed in turn as they were forced to their knees like Khellus. Favriel begged Asmoran to stop this madness, that they'd do anything to prove their loyalty... anything to live.

"Khellus!" Abrodail cried, tears streaking her face. "Do something! Gods, please!"

Chapter 4

He struggled in place, but the guards held him as surely as iron manacles. Ensnared and disarmed, he could only watch as swords were poised over the couple's backs, aimed at their hearts.

He bellowed over the rising chaos. "Listen to me, Asmoran. I swear these two are loyal to you. Killing them is pointless. Don't do this."

Asmoran didn't so much as glance his way. He remained staring at the couple, looking sorrowful at having to eliminate valuable servants like a hunter putting down a pair of rabid dogs. Eogwen beat her wooden fork against the guard holding her in place, but he didn't flinch.

At the noble's gesture, the swords plunged down in unison. They thrust into Abrodail and Favriel's backs and out through their chests.

Khellus roared. Eogwen screamed. Their cries rose and mingled, a chorus of horror and loss. The couple jerked on the blades for a few moments, mouths gaping. Then their twitching ceased and all tension fled their bodies. They slumped off the blades as one, flopping to lie beside each other, blood running together. Abrodail's glazed eyes stared over at Khellus, damning him for his helplessness.

Sobs shook Eogwen and she thrashed in her guard's grip. Asmoran came over and took her, holding her shoulders until she exhausted her efforts and stood distraught and drained.

"Little flower," Asmoran knelt and took Eogwen's hands in his own. "Your parents' deaths are this man's fault." He nodded at Khellus. "He forced them to disobey me, and that forced me to kill them. He is the monster here, not me. Someday, you will understand this."

He rose and tugged her toward the front room. "Now come along. You've seen enough bloodshed for one night. Let's leave this villain to his fate. I believe there is some roast duck waiting for us down in the dining hall." Asmoran glanced at Khellus' captors. "I trust you can see him as cleanly dispatched as you did these two?" He nudged Favriel with a velvet slipper.

The grip on Khellus' arms tightened and the guards clustered closer.

"Yessuh," said one.

Asmoran exited, dragging a crying Eogwen behind. The guards who'd executed Abrodail and Favriel trailed them, leaving Khellus still with half a dozen to contend with.

Before he could settle on any particular plan, a clout to the back of his head sent his vision spinning. Rough hands hauled him upright and slammed him against a wall. By the time the room settled, three crossbowmen had lined up opposite him, quarrels aimed at this head and heart. One guard stood a couple steps to his left, sword raised, two on his right, similarly readied. No escape. No more than a few moments left to live.

Khellus's mind raced as he considered a few frantic options. Charge them and hope he took a quarrel in a non-vital spot? Hope for miraculously bad aim and try to appropriate one of the blades, slaying them all with abandon?

Or did he accept that death had come for him at last? He'd dealt it out so often with mindless ruthlessness. He'd lived as the king's blade for so many years, rarely considering the consequences of his actions beyond the duty he performed. Now those consequences lay dripping blood onto the stones. They were being yanked down a hall, screaming for a mother and father who'd never answer again.

Khellus focused on his executioners and straightened his spine. Might as well meet his end with a measure of courage.

Then one of the guards winked, turned, and fired a bolt into the head of the guard beside him.

As the rest of the guards spun and gawped at this, Khellus dove at the swordsman on his left. The third crossbowman fired, but the quarrel ricocheted over Khellus's shoulder. The swordsman turned, trying to cut up, but Khellus snagged the man's wrist and spun, driving the man face-first into the wall. The sword dropped, but he snatched it up before it hit the floor.

A chop across the back of the neck cut his assailant's head free from his body as Khellus fell into a fighting stance as the other swordsmen advanced. The treacherous guard was using his crossbow like a club, bludgeoning the last crossbowman over the head until he dropped.

The two remaining guards paused in mid-charge, uncertain which man to attack first. Khellus exchanged a look with his unexpected helper. Groxley grinned back at him from under a guard's helm. He wore the full uniform, though Khellus noted a few discrepancies... such as the blood stain down one side and a few gouged leather panels.

"You."

"Me." Groxley grinned wider. "Wanna show these louts what real fightin's like?"

They each fixed on one of the swordsmen, who looked grim and determined to battle to the death. Groxley continued using the crossbow like a mace, driving his target back with brute force. Khellus had no difficulty slapping aside his opponent's desperate attacks.

After several brief clashes, the swordsman turned and tried to run. However, Khellus lunged and pierced him in the lower back. The man stiffened and fell. Khellus stepped in and ended him with a slash across the throat.

He turned just as Groxley caved in his opponent's skull with a brutal blow. Fresher blood now spattered his leather armour. The two killers eyed each other over the corpses.

"You were here all along," Khellus said.

"Well, not more than a coupla hours," Groxley said. "Caught a guard taking a piss as he was goin' off duty last night. He wouldn't be missed 'till tomorrow, so I stashed 'im, took his gear, and came in to watch the fun when you tried to give the lord his due." He glanced around the room, amused. "Sure didn't figure I'd wind up helpin' stop you. Gotta say, I'm a little disappointed. You gettin' caught so easily."

Khellus thrust his sword at the bodies of Abrodail and Favriel. "You could've stopped him. Stopped him from killing them."

"What? And spoil the surprise? Why would I go and do that? Was a good bit of fun seein' them begging for their lives. Like little kitties, mewlin' and wrigglin' until they got gutted good. Plus seein' you getting all broken up over them. Didn't think you was such a feather-hearted bitch."

Khellus scowled. Blood thumped in his ears as his fury rose at the other man's heartless cruelty. But had he been any better when he'd singled out Abrodail and made her an unwilling accomplice? The couple lay dead just as much thanks to him as Groxley's indifference. "Then why bother saving me?"

"'Cause you didn't deserve to die that way." Groxley wiped a dribble of blood off his armour and sucked it from his fingers. "I can respect another professional, y'know? So here's what I's gonna do. Since you's so sad to see your friends lose their heads, I'll snap yours off as well an let you find 'em in the misty paths, where you can spend all eternity apologizin' for being such a bad, bad man. That's the death you deserve. Then... " He licked his lips. "Then I'm gonna go down, finish the job you bungled, and take the lil' girl and have a bit of fun with 'er before making her squeal like her folks did."

Khellus roared as he attacked. Groxley's grin didn't waver as he flung the crossbow, forcing Khellus to weave aside. When he righted, Groxley had retrieved a sword of his own. Their blades clanged as they tested each other's guard.

Khellus cut low and then blocked a vicious cut at his side. He caught an overhead blow, but Groxley snapped a leg up and into his chest. He stumbled back against the wall and whirled aside as Groxley's sword struck sparks off the stones.

They circle each other, shuffling over the bodies and avoiding the pools of blood along the floor. Groxley lacked Khellus's fluidity and speed, but made up for it with a ferocity that seemed inhumanly strong. He battered the assassin's defences, forcing him to divert all his strength and focus into keeping the strikes from connecting.

Khellus dashed in and out of range, stabbing and slashing when he could spare the effort. He left the thug bleeding from several shallow wounds, but Groxley acted no more affected than if he'd been tickled. All the while, Groxley kept his grin fixed like death's own visage.

As the fight moved around the room, Groxley started wielding the sword with one hand while snatching up random objects and flinging them with the other. Khellus dodged a marble bust, which shattered against the wall. Asmoran's inkwell and pitcher of wine splashed past, casting droplets across his face. Groxley even tore the helm off his own head and whipped it out to clang against the stones.

Khellus ground his teeth, determined to not let the man distract him. Then Groxley threw his sword like a spear. Khellus spun to let it pass by. As he reoriented, a body filled his vision. Groxley had stooped and scooped up Abrodail's corpse, which he'd flung straight at Khellus.

Khellus lurched aside, but the body still slammed into his shoulder. Thrown off-balance, he stumbled and braced a hand on the floor. He tried to raise the sword, but Groxley knocked it aside, taking another cut on the forearm as he did. He grabbed the hilt and tore it loose from Khellus's hand, tossing the blade aside.

Long, absurdly strong fingers wrapped around Khellus's throat, squeezing as they drove him down. Khellus grabbed for purchase, tried to tear the hands away, but they remained fixed as surely as iron clamps. Groxley pressed all his weight on top of the assassin, grinding the back of his skull against stone.

"Give 'em my regards," Groxley said.

Khellus snapped blows up into the man's face, cracking a cheekbone and mashing his nose. Yet the thug didn't flinch. Khellus strained for breath even as his vision started to blur and grey around the edges. He tried to jab fingers into Groxley's eyes, but the man jerked back, laughing, just out of reach.

Khellus slid one hand around in search of anything he could use as a weapon. His sight narrowed to focus on Groxley's hideous grin and strength began to seep from him. Just then, his fingers connected with a small blunt object.

Eogwen's wooden fork. She must've dropped it when Asmoran hauled her off.

He snatched the fork up and rammed it up and into Groxley's right socket. The man howled and lurched back, hands going to cover the wounded eye. Khellus sucked in precious air as he somersaulted backwards and up to his feet. He recovered the sword and dashed in, driving the blade through the thug's chest.

Groxley screamed and clutched the blade as if trying to drag it back out. Blood poured from his fingers, but he refused to let go. He bared teeth at Khellus and sputtered as crimson bubbles frothed his lips.

"That... that wasn't... "

Whatever final insult or defiance he intended went unfinished as his grin finally slipped off his face. He sagged on the blade. Khellus planted a boot on his chest to force him off, casting him aside like the trash he was. Then he surveyed the corpse-strewn room, trying to sort his thoughts through a haze of unexpected fury.

As an assassin, he'd always remained aloof from his victims, never invested in their fate beyond his role in ending their lives. It often didn't matter who he killed or why, so long as he did so under the king's command. Remaining focused within a fight... keeping the killing impersonal... taking time to plot out every step of the execution... all these things had helped him complete dozens of jobs over the years with aplomb.

This time, though, was different. In his haste, he'd let things get personal. He'd thought himself able to withstand the tug of old emotion, able to consider Abrodail as just a valuable resource he could exploit without consequence.

He'd been wrong.

Asmoran still needed to die, but Khellus felt a new sense of commitment in the act. The noble had his daughter. *His daughter.* It didn't matter that he hadn't known of her existence until just earlier in the day. She was his flesh and blood, and now another sought to abuse such.

Crossing the room, he knelt by Abrodail and brushed hair away from her slack face. Kissing her forehead, he whispered, "Forgive me, Abby. You deserved a far better fate than this. I swear this, though. Eogwen will be cared for. She will be raised to defend herself so no one not even me can ever hurt her again."

Rising, he went over to a fallen guard and retrieved a second blade. The guards had taken his usual swords, but he'd long ago learned to fight with whatever weapon fate offered him in the moment. One edge could cut just as well as another.

Possessed now of a singular purpose, Khellus strode from the room and out into the main hall. The marble busts lining this stretch stared at him with dead eyes, as if in judgment, but he passed by their gazes and only paused when he reached the top of the stairs.

"Asmoran!" His voice echoed through the tower depths. "Prepare yourself!"

He smiled to himself as footsteps tromped up until several guards appeared at the landing below. They looked shocked to see him alive, but then charged up to meet him. Impressed by their loyalty and courage, Khellus slew them as quickly as he could. One man fell missing half his skull. Another gushed blood from a severed arm. The third clutched a sucking gut wound.

Khellus left them writhing in his wake as he descended. Faint shouts came from further down, and he assumed an alarm had been raised. Excellent.

Guards rushed him straight on. Others waited around corners, aiming to ambush. Others ran off calling for reinforcements. He left some dead, some bleeding out, others crippled with broken knees or arms. Their screams of pain and fear filled the tower the further he went.

Was this what Groxley once felt when he paved a path in mangled flesh and spilled blood? This morbid pleasure of dispatching one enemy after the next, of knowing one less person stood between him and his ultimate victim? A strange feeling swelled within him with each guard dispatched. Not contentment or happiness, but a growing satisfaction of using his skills to eliminate any obstacle. He'd thought himself so different from the thuggish killer, yet now might as well have tread in his very footsteps.

At last, he took down two guards and marched through the doorway they'd been posted at. The dining hall held ten long tables, able to hold hundreds of people. Enormous fireplaces lined the walls, all dead except for the one at the far end.

There, Asmoran sat at the head table, a greasy duck breast being shredded between his plump fingers. Eogwen sat across from him, staring at a plate piled high with meat, fruit, and sweetbreads.

The noble rose at Khellus's entrance. "I'd prefer my dinner not be spoiled."

A band of five guards emerged from the shadows and headed Khellus's way.

"You should've run," Khellus said.

"Be routed out from my own home by a brute like yourself?" Asmoran huffed. "Nonsense. This will be entertaining."

Khellus walked straight up the aisle between the tables as the guards spread out to come at him from all angles. Asmoran watched, looking anticipatory of the violent show.

Two guards drove in on his right, attempting to push him into reach of the other three. Khellus deflected a strike and his riposte left a guard clutching his shoulder. The other kept his distance, trying to distract him with constant feints.

Sensing the others rushing at his back, Khellus swivelled and let a swipe slice air inches from his face. Khellus flipped over backwards and landed on top of one of the dining tables. Blades cut at his legs, and he jumped over the attacks, lashing out at their heads in return.

A blow clipped one of the guards across the temple and sent him staggering. One guard tried to jump up and meet him on equal levels. As he set a foot on the bench, Khellus struck his sword aside and kicked out. His heel smashed into the guard's face, crunching bone and cartilage.

Khellus jumped down, but on the other side of the table, forcing the remaining guards to split up as they came at him again. One rushed around either end while the third clambered up onto the table he'd just vacated. Before his companions could get back in range, Khellus surged back up onto the bench and rammed his sword through the table-climber's bowels. Shrieking, the guard toppled back and flopped to the floor.

The last two attacked Khellus from either side. He wielded both swords in tandem, blocking their simultaneous strikes. A kick to one guard's stomach gave him enough time to sweep around and strike the other's head off. Then he spun through the momentum, caught the last guard's frantic slash with one sword and plunged the other through the man's ribs. Gurgling his last, the guard fell away.

Thumping footsteps jerked Khellus's attention to where Asmoran ran for a side door, Eogwen in tow. He sprinted that way, vaulted a table, and threw himself into the noble's path. As Khellus intercepted them, Asmoran swept Eogwen up and held her against his chest. A paring knife appeared in his hand and he pressed his against her throat, dimpling the skin.

Khellus hesitated just one step away from striking range.

Asmoran's jiggling cheeks creased in a smirk. "Shall we wait for more of my men to arrive?" he asked, "or would you like me to bleed her now?"

Khellus glanced at Eogwen.

"Shut your eyes," he told her.

"No."

He met her stare. Whatever tears she'd shed earlier had dried, leaving her face scrunched in determination. A smile twitched the corner of his mouth.

"Well then? What're you waiting for girl?"

Eogwen grabbed one of Asmoran's fingers, raised it to her mouth, and bit hard. Asmoran jerked and hollered. Before he could drive the knife home, Khellus skewered the hand holding it. His blade shot just over Eogwen's shoulder and pinned Asmoran's arm to his own body.

The noble squalled and stumbled back, trying to shake the sword loose as it stuck out from his chest. Eogwen fell from his grasp, and Khellus snatched her in mid-air with his free hand and pulled her in close. Frail arms wrapped around his neck as he kept his other sword pointed at Asmoran.

Asmoran backed up until he struck the door he'd been aiming to escape through. His whole body trembled. "Wait. I can pay you magnificently. I can"

Bored by the pathetic pleas, Khellus thrust the sword through the man's sagging throat and into the wood on the other side. The noble died upright, choking on his own gore, .

The whole while, Eogwen held Khellus tight. Once Asmoran stopped squirming, he turned away and carried Eogwen from the hall. His slaughter through the tower must've severely depleted the number of guards on duty, for they met none as they emerged into the crisp night air. He carried her through an empty courtyard and into the garden on the west side of the estate. Once hidden among the thick hedges, he paused and set her down.

Eogwen looked as if she wanted to dart off, but she remained rooted in place, dress clutched in her fists. "Are you gonna kill me too?" she asked.

"Would I have rescued you if I'd planned to do that?"

Her voice wavered slightly. "Why didn't you rescue my mommy and daddy?"

Khellus crouched to meet her at eye level. "I wish I could have, but you can't rescue everyone all the time. Your mother was a very brave woman. Are you brave like her?"

She nodded.

"Good. Because what comes next is going to require you to be very brave. We're going to leave here, understand? Forever. I'm taking you with me and going to look after you until you can look after yourself."

"Why?"

"I promised your mother I would."

Her mouth pinched. "I don't like you."

"I know. You can hate me if you want. I won't blame you. But I can teach you how to be strong. How to fight so that men like him..." He jabbed a thumb back toward the hall where Asmoran's corpse hung, stuck to the door. " ...can't ever threaten you again. Do you want that?"

Eogwen looked to the northwestern tower for a long moment. He didn't doubt her thoughts fixated on her mother and father's bodies up in the tower. She'd be in shock for a good while, and he'd have to deal with the fallout should she choose to blame him for their deaths. Whether or not she eventually accepted him as her true father would remain to be seen—but he was prepared to handle the consequences either way. Time for him to take true responsibility for his actions. He'd made his choices, for good or ill, and now had to pay the price.

Turning her back to the manor, she reached out and grabbed his hand. Khellus allowed himself the slightest smile, and then led her deeper into the garden, where they could seek out the nearest wall and climb over to freedom.

Like a pair of living shadows, they glided along noiselessly and vanished into the night.

The End

About the Author

Author and editor Josh Vogt's work covers fantasy, science fiction, horror, humor, pulp, and more. His debut fantasy novel is Pathfinder Tales: Forge of Ashes, alongside the launch of his urban fantasy series, The Cleaners, with Enter the Janitor and The Maids of Wrath. He's an editor at Paizo, a Scribe Award finalist, and a member of both SFWA and the International Association of Media Tie-In Writers. Find him at JRVogt.com or on Twitter @JRVogt.

The Fall and Redemption of Davaldion

By

Craig Teal

Chapter 1

Damitri hid amongst the shadows against the black granite walls of the cultist's lair. Slowly he shifted on the balls of his feet, moving through the darkness as he made his way to the overhang he had spied on his descent.

He hoped that from the raised vantage point he would be able to get a clear view of the horrors that awaited him below and, more importantly, come up with a way to destroy them. Damitri hated this part; it was always the same - he would be told of the appearance of a demon or worse and asked to go and deal with it. *Deal with it*, he thought to himself *if only they understood*, for he knew what was to come and it never was a simple matter of dealing with it.

Lowering his hood Damitri listened for any approaching guards, comfortable that he was alone he slipped from his hiding spot into the torch lit corridor, the soft light illuminated his pale skin and unearthly angular features as he climbed to the top of the overhang. After taking precautions to remain hidden, he peered over the edge into the dark chamber below.

The head of the cult stood triumphant before his followers. The golden symbol of a demon prince on his chest seemed to glow in the dark, it was a symbol that Damitri knew better than he would have liked. "Na'Kraken" he whispered.

"My children," the dark priest said, his voice carrying a honeyed tone, "our moment of triumph is upon us and soon our lord shall walk freely amongst us."

Damitri had heard enough, he knew he needed to act swiftly and dropped into the chamber below, reaching within himself he called upon his innate ability to slip into the realm of shadow as he faded from view. The dark priest, unaware of the events above him, drew forth a sacrificial blade as he recited a dark prayer; "Hear me our dark lord as we ca--" His prayer, was cut short as a silvered blade suddenly arced through his body as the dark cloaked figure of Damitri flickered into view before the congregation.

The cultists stood stunned for a moment as the priest made a final gurgled groan as his body fell apart. "Leave this place and never return," came Damitri's only warning. He hoped and prayed that they would listen, but he knew they were just farmers and villagers who had been led astray with empty promises of a better life; and deep down he knew they were too far gone.

The nearest three cultists screamed their dark benefactors name and charged, their spears pointed ahead of them. With a heavy heart Damitri quickly brought his sword to bear. There was a ring of steel on steel as Damitri quickly overpowered these first attackers; disarming one, dismembering the second and beheading the third. More of the cultists entered the fray and he quickly spun, letting an attacker pass him whilst deflecting a second spear with his sword. Another's eyes widened as Damitri grabbed his spear and lifted it, allowing him to quickly disembowel him.

With the cult's leader and several of its guard's dead at the heretic's feet the remaining cultists found their faith shaken and backed away, fearfully.

Damitri, noting their hesitation, took the initiative and the last few steps to the altar where after scanning the stunned crowd he called upon the magic of the goddess Shi'Ara the light warden to cleanse the shrine.

Concentrating, a faint glow began to envelop his empty hand which soon became a ball of radiant light. "Your cult is ended," he shouted as he released the spell. A wave of brilliance briefly illuminated the walls of the dark temple; the more corrupt of the cultists felt their skin burn and crack as the altar to Na'Kraken shattered in a shower of gold and black stone.

Damitri hadn't noticed that another of the cult's guards had a crossbow and was struggling to blink away the bright light as he tried to place Damitri squarely in his sights. Just as he was about to let loose his bolt a firm hand grabbed and dragged him into the shadows. "Not today," a voice close at his ear said coldly, "he is not yours to take".

The cultist's eyes bulged as the speaker bit deep into his neck; his scream of anguish fell unheard into the very shadows he was drawn into.

As the light faded the remaining cultists, with the cult master's hold on them fading, scurried away to their farms and homesteads.

Damitri watched them leave and was comforted that he had needed to kill so few; he only hoped that they would remember and make better use of the time the gods had given them.

He headed down the mountainside. Finally, with his mission complete, he could return home.

Damitri's benefactor watched with interest "until next time, Son of Decar," he said smiling before he stepped back into the darkness.

***

A week later Damitri was called into the ante chamber of high priest Galewyn, which made him uneasy: "Why does he need me again so soon?" he pondered. As always following a successful removal of a cult the other cults would quickly go to ground which would make his work harder.

Damitri collected his thoughts and knocked politely. A moment later the wizened face of Galewyn greeted him through the opened door: "Ah Damitri my boy, please come in." Once Damitri took his seat Galewyn explained, "it appears the forces of the Fallen are seeking a whitelighter."

Damitri raised an eyebrow. "There have been no whitelighters in over a hundred years!".

"That is not entirely accurate" Galewyn admitted.

Damitri was taken aback "What do you mean 'not entirely accurate?'"

"I mean that there have not been any whitelighters until recently."

"WHAT?" Damitri shot to his feet, "you said you would tell me when they returned"

"And THAT is just what I am doing now, so sit down. Now before you interrupt again, let me answer the inevitable." Galewyn let out a sigh and passed Damitri a scroll from his desk: "Yes she has, no she's doesn't and yes you may." Galewyn smiled at the shock on Damitri's face as the questions swimming inside his head were quickly answered.

"How did you know what I was going to say?" he asked, puzzled.

"Because you always ask the same three questions," Galewyn replied with a smile. "The details of where you need to go and what you need to do are written in the scroll, you leave today," Galewyn stood up indicating their meeting was over. Damitri climbed to his feet and asked softly "does this have to end the same way again?"

Galewyn took a moment to consider before answering "as always that will depend on her."

With a gentle bow Damitri turned and left the chamber. *Finally*, he thought. *After a hundred years he was finally going to see her again.* Damitri smiled.

Galewyn watched: "And so the cycle begins again," he spoke out loud and walked to a large ornate silver mirror that hung upon the wall and placed his fingers gently upon the glass. "Soon it will be time, my brothers," his voice heavy with a hidden sadness.

The surface of the mirror seemed to shimmer and shift as a single voice responded: "The shadow shifts and the stars have begun to come out, we will be ready brother." The mirror became still again and Galewyn was alone, his thoughts on Damitri's task and what the man had to endure yet again. Galewyn did not envy him.

Chapter 2

It took Damitri several days to reach the valley that housed the village of Hiltram. He hurried down the mountainside, wary of the coming evening and the fiends that it could bring. He also wished his arrival into town to be as subtle as possible.

It didn't take long for him to find his destination. Following his instructions he found himself standing before an inn named the *Unicorn and Boar* and, after gathering his wits, he entered, pausing slightly at the doorway to remind himself that she wouldn't remember him.

The inn itself was typical for the region, a large bar ran down the side with several iron bound barrels stacked behind. A bearlike man that Damitri knew all too well stood behind the bar cleaning an iron flagon, "Wulfren" Damitri smiled to himself , after catching his friend's eye he deftly moved past several groups of rowdy youths and townsfolk before settling at an empty table by the side of the bar.

Well, I'm here, he thought to himself, *so where are you?* He scanned the bar looking for a face he had not seen for nearly a hundred years.

He was distracted by a young barmaid who smiled politely and placed a flagon of ale on his table. He could see the freshness of youth as her face reddened before she stuttered. "My father thought you would like this after your long trip." *Father* Damitri thought, looking past the barmaid to the barman, who this time nodded to him. "Thank you young lady, it is greatly appreciated." His remark made her giggle and she quickly disappeared amongst the revellers in the inn. Had it really been that long already? Rosie had been a child when he had last seen her.

Damitri nursed the flagon in front of him for a moment before a shadow loomed above him and he found himself looking up into the barman's dark eyes.

"I got word that you had been sent my way." His voice was a low whisper.

"It's been a while, Wulfren," Damitri said smiling as he raised his drink to his friend who tapped his flagon to Damitri's, "Rosie has definitely grown up," he continued as he looked at the young barmaid as she mingled among the patrons of the inn. Wulfren smiled: "That's not Rosie, that's Rosie's daughter Serra" Damitri almost felt his eyes pop out of his head. "What! How long has it been?" His reaction made the large man laugh heartily. "You're a man out of time, Damitri, and that is one of the things I do not envy of you." He settled his flagon back on the table, "it's been nearly twenty five years since we fought together on the plains of Dunmbar" A moment passed

"Really that long? I thought you had just aged badly," a smile crossing both their faces at the younger looking man's quip.

"I'd be careful, this ox is not past its prime just yet." They laughed again for a moment then the barman's face became dark. He slowly reached forward and gripped Damitri's forearm with his hand: "They know she is here."

"Damn it," Damitri spat, "there goes my advantage."

The barman removed his hand and settled back in his chair.

"How long have they been here?" Damitri asked. "A day or so ago, I arranged for her to stay in the inn at what she believes to be her father's request to learn more about the townsfolk."

After reflecting on the barman's actions, he asked, "is the inn warded?"

The barman smiled. "You wound me, son of D'mar" he laughed, "aye, the inn is warded with the best I could muster but it won't hold them back forever." Wulfren climbed back to his feet: "Come with me and I'll introduce you to her," he paused to surpress a laugh, "be warned, she is a tad disagreeable about her father's decision. I do not envy your task."

"Why, thank you for the warning," Damitri retorted. He hated this part.

The barman led Damitri up to the second floor and down a candle lit landing to a doorway where two swordsmen sat at a table playing dice. Upon seeing Damitri they climbed to their feet. "Easy lads, this is the one I said was coming to relieve you of your burden."

"About bloody time," the first of the guards stated as they quickly grabbed their things and disappeared down the hallway.

"I hope you're ready for this lad," Wulfren laughed as he knocked on the door.

"Who is it?" a sharp reply rang out.

"It's Wulfren, M' lady, I have a guest who wishes to speak with you," he politely replied.

"Doesn't he know what time it is, I'm hardly prepared to entertain, don't you think?" the voice replied through the door.

Damitri noticed the barman flinch and smiled as he watched the large man struggle to keep his composure.

"A thousand pardons M' lady, but this visitor is here at your father's request."

A moment passed and they heard a commotion behind the door. "Very well," she sighed, "just give me a moment."

"Her father's request!" Damitri whispered.

"I improvised," the barman said grinning.

A noise brought their attention back to the door, which opened to reveal a young woman dressed in her nightdress with a turquoise robe wrapped around her shoulders. Her long, dark, curled hair framed her face, she was as beautiful as he remembered her, even though at this point in time her pale green eyes were narrowed in a scowl that would have cowed the fiercest of trolls.

"So, what is it?" she asked coldly, her hands on her hips.

"I will take my leave," the barman said and, with a slight bow, he turned and headed back down the landing.

Damitri watched the barman leave and could have sworn he heard him chuckle. He turned to find the maiden's green eyes burning into him. "Well?" she asked, her tone even colder than before.

"M' lady please pardon this intrusion at this hour but I must talk with you at the utmost urgency," Damitri explained.

"And what could possibly warrant my attention at this hour?" she asked.

"Your safety, M' lady" Damitri replied.

His response caught her off guard and for a moment she lost her composure: "And you say my father sent you?" Damitri simply nodded. She groaned and, after taking a step to the side, gestured into the room, "then I guess you better come inside."

Damitri entered and upon hearing the door close he turned to find the maiden stood with her back to the door, a loaded crossbow in her hand: "I suggest you talk quickly," she said.

"Please, you won't be needing that," Damitri said calmly as he lifted his hands.

"I'll be the judge of that," she tightened her grip on the trigger, "so tell me, why are you here?"

Damitri thought quickly: he could disarm her but that wouldn't help him earn her trust, or alternatively he could continue the story of her father requesting his aid, though her actions told him she doubted its legitimacy. Even though he could easily withstand the bolt if it hit him, he would rather not have to explain that to her just yet. In the end Damitri decided that a half-truth would serve him better than a lie.

"My apologies, M' lady," Damitri said soothingly as he bowed, "I did not wish to alarm you with the news I bring." He took another step towards the fire. "It was true that your safety is paramount to me, though your father is not completely aware of who is hunting you." He turned and moved to the window, as the barman had said it was adorned with a selection of warding runes. He waved his hand across them feeling the strength of the magic; which surprised him. *So Wulfren has learnt some new tricks,* he thought to himself.

"M' lady you were brought away from your home and comforts for a reason." He gestured to the runes that adorned the window frames: "These runes are designed to keep those that are unwelcome out."

"And who might they be," she scoffed.

"I hope you never find out." The solemnness of his response took her aback. "Needless to say," he continued, "tomorrow I will escort you to Reul Na Maidne where I will be able to explain."

"If you think I am travelling with you, then you are very much mistaken," her hand tightening around the trigger of the hand bow, "you think that you can come here and tell me that my life is in danger and expect me to go running north with you at the drop of a hat, do you think I'm a child?" She thrust her hand forward, hand bow pointed at his heart, "and rest assured, my father will be told of this."

Shi'Ara why do you hate me? Damitri thought to himself as he tried to reason with her.

***

As Damitri argued over the journey a band of men appeared on a nearby hill; their cracked black leather-like skin only distinguishable from their armour by the way they moved. As they reached the top of the hill the air seemed to shift as a lone figure stepped from the realm of shadow where he had lain hidden.

"You called for us?" the largest of the men said.

"Indeed I did," the figure responded "the one you seek is at the inn, you will be expected and she is well guarded." He threw open his cloak revealing the ivory hilts of twin swords hung from his waist. "Your task is a simple one, bring the girl to me alive" he pointed to one of the larger men "and untouched. Do what you want with the rest, now be gone." With that the band descended the hill towards the unsuspecting village.

***

Wulfren stood behind his bar, a vigilant eye on his granddaughter as she moved amongst the tables. He turned to reach for another mug when he caught sight of the candle that sat upon the bar. The flame had turned green. His blood ran cold and he quickly reached beneath the bar.

Damitri was making little progress with the stubborn heiress when the sound of raised voices downstairs caught his attention. He opened the door to see Wulfren heading towards them, a large twin bladed axe in his hand. His expression told Damitri all he needed to know.

"How many?" Damitri asked.

"I'm not sure," Wulfren replied "they haven't tried to enter the inn… yet."

Damitri turned to the maiden: "we're out of time," he pleaded, "we need to go n--" His sentence was cut short as a figure flew towards the window.

The wards that had been carved there suddenly burst into life as a blast of perfect light flooded the room, blinding them for a just a moment. When the light dimmed, all that remained of their attacker was a smouldering grey ash.

Damitri grabbed the girl. "We're leaving!" he shouted, her eyes widening as the reality of the situation hit her. "We need to leave, they will kill everyone nearby if it helps them get at you." Turning to Wulfren he asked "where's Serra?"

"She's taken those who are unable to fight into the basement; it is well warded."

Damitri quickly gathered a travelling dress and some boots and thrust them into her hands: "Get dressed." She started to complain but his expression brooked no argument.

She quickly dressed herself, trying to cover her embarrassment as Damitri moved to the window. He saw several figures move away from the dim illumination, now aware of the threat.

Looking over his shoulder he could see her slipping on her boots. "How many swords do we have?" Damitri asked.

"Seven," came Wulfren's stoic reply.

Damitri took a moment to contemplate his next move. "We can't stay here," he said. "As soon as they realise they can't gain entry, they will burn the inn down and kill everyone inside." "You're surely not suggesting you run!" Wulfren said, taking a tighter grip on his axe.

"If we stay, they will wear us down before the dawn; if we run we will at least have a chance of out-running them."

"I'm not going out there with those things." The maiden said.

Damitri firmly grabbed her arm and turned her to face the fire: "Do you see the green flames?" the anger clear in his voice, "this is the sign that there is an evil waiting outside that you cannot begin to comprehend, and if they can't get at you, they will send for something that can."

He turned her to face him. "If they get you they will do far more than just hurt or kill, they will make you watch as they murder and violate every other person they find alive in this inn. We have to go, it's the only way to save them." He released her arm and collected her hand bow.

"Do you know how to use this?" he said passing it to her, his voice calm again. She nodded "Good, I think you will have use for it before this night is through."

Turning to Wulfren he motioned to the corridor. "Let's be off."

"How do you expect to get away?" the large man asked.

"I was hoping that you would provide me with a diversion," Damitri said with a subtle smile.

The large man laughed: "I think I have something in mind."

The two men and the reluctant maiden descended the stairs into the bar room, where several armed men and Serra awaited them.

"Damn it lass, I told you to wait inside the basement."

"But what about you, Grumpy?"

His demeanour softened. "I'll be fine lass, but I'll need my focus to get us out of this and I can't do that if I'm worrying about you." He put his hand on her delicate face and wiped away her tears. "I'll be down in a bit when it's all over, I promise."

"You promise?"

"Of course," he replied, she reluctantly turned and headed down to the basement, looking back once at her grandfather before she disappeared from view.

Thankful of the brief distraction Damitri asked the maiden: "before we do this might I know your name?" she looked hatefully at him for a moment before replying, "Lady Selina of Rorickstead."

"Then Selina of Rorickstead, I guess it is time for us to go."

Wulfren was chanting something to his axe, which burst into a silvered light. "Are you ready?" Damitri asked.

"As I'll ever be," the axeman said as he placed his hand on his shoulder. "I'll be seeing you," and moved to the door, a couple of swordsmen to his side.

"Let's go," Damitri said as he offered his hand to Selina.

The figures that circled the inn waited for their master. Murlac tested the wards that blocked their access and spat; he would have burned the inn down if he had not needed her intact and now he had been forced to report his delay, the punishment for which he did not relish.

"Murlac" the disembodied voice called out, catching his attention and he turned to find the figure of his master slowly manifested from the night behind him. "Why do you not have the girl?" The ice in his voice cut through the blackened exterior of the killer and he trembled on the spot. "The inn is warded my master, we cannot gain entry without damage to ourselves or risk to the girl," he feebly replied.

The pale hand of the dark robed figure shot forward at the man's throat and Murlac found himself choking as his body was lifted into the air.

"I have little time for excuses, Murlac. You and your men are expendable, so get me the girl." He dropped the trembling figure to the ground and move towards the inn doors, which suddenly opened. In the doorway stood a giant figure wielding an axe that glowed with a silver light.

The giant's voice rang out: "Begone, these people are not for you." Several of Murlac's men quickly moved towards the now open doorway when the giant's voice rang out again. "Begone I say for this inn is protected," and with that his free hand burst into silver fire that caused the figures to draw back. "**An cèitean** na solas gabh sibh." His words were firm and loaded with purpose as the silver fire that engulfed his hand seemed to suddenly dim, causing the figures to run forward once again, the giant grinned "now burn!" he roared as he thrust his hand forward; a burst of silver fire flew from his hands and enveloped the entire inn with streaks of light emanating from the windows, quickly turning the charging men to ash.

A similar fate would have been granted to Murlac had he not thrown himself behind his master, for although the spell was powerful he was not powerless to resist it, and the magic split around him as water splits around a rock in a river.

Wulfran was taken by surprise that the figure could withstand the spell but it had served its purpose and allowed Damitri the window of opportunity that he required; every moment that he could give him from this point on was a bonus; "Have at thee!" he roared as he flew towards the figure before him.

His first blow was to gauge his opponent, who quickly ducked his blow and circled behind him drawing a spiral horn hilted sword. Wulfran attacked again, their weapons ringing as the cloaked figure time and time again matched his blows and turned them aside.

Deciding a change of pace was needed, Wulfran struck at his opponent's weapon and when they turned to avoid the blow his arm shot out grabbing the defender's flailing cloak, quickly turning and dragging him off balance before throwing him to the side. The dark warrior quickly recovered and rolled with the throw, swiftly returning to his feet.

Murlac, seizing the opportunity, charged at the large man and slashed him across his shoulder, causing a roar of pain from the large figure. His audacity was rewarded with a swift back fist that spun Murlac on the spot as the large axe removed his head from his shoulders, his body quickly turning to black ash.

Clutching his shoulder Wulfran quickly turned to the remaining dark warrior who stood still for a moment, almost sniffing the air. "A clever gambit lightwarden, but your ruse is up." He took a step back: "Take relish in your victory, for the war will be over by the coming dawn," and with that the figure faded into the vary darkness of the night.

Wulfren quickly returned to the safety of the inn, where he began to comprehend the finality of the warrior's words. "Prove them wrong, Damitri, prove them wrong," he prayed.

Chapter 3

Selina's heart pounded as she ran through the forest, her arm outstretched as her guardian Damitri guided her through the thick undergrowth.

"Quickly," he hissed, "they are gaining on us." His warning rang true as two of their pursuers sprang from the undergrowth, their obsidian blades glowing with a purple fire. Yet for all their cunning their ambush was for nought, as Damitri quickly threw Selina to the ground before drawing his own silvered blade in a swift arc. Such a sense of honed purpose and precision, it caused the attackers to freeze in their steps as the first of Damitri's assailants' heads fell from his shoulders, and the second could only stare down at the long silvered blade that now protruded from his chest.

Withdrawing his blade Damitri quickly sheathed it as the remaining swordsman fell to the ground. His eyes quickly darted to the surrounding trees before returning to Selina, who was staggering back to her feet. "You killed them," she said her voice shaking.

"I am your guardian, we all have a purpose m'lady," came his stoic response. Their brief respite was quickly broken by the sounds of a large beast in the distance. "Come," Damitri soothed as he offered his hand. "There are many more behind us."

As they started to make their way again she whispered to him, "why do they want me so badly?" "Because M'lady, they fear your purpose." He slowed and turned to face her, a look of confusion on her face. "I promise I will explain everything to you as soon as we're safe." He turned from her again and resumed his pace: "If we can make the edge of the forest by daybreak, we have a chance."

Damitri knew that if he was alone, escaping would be easy. Vastly outnumbered, he was fearful of his charge falling into the hands of the lords that dwelt below the black and twisted forest of Ur.

A swift movement to his left brought his attention back to the situation at hand and he quickly spun on the heel of his boot as a black barbed arrow grazed him across his cheek before striking the tree next to him. He quickly led Selina through the trees to his right and, as he became aware of their pursuers behind them he realised he was being coerced into a specific path until finally he found himself staring at a group of those that were following him, the Nightfell marauders.

Damitri's hand flew to his hilt when a deep voice rang out, a voice that Damitri knew too well. "Enough of this," the voice thundered as a tall figure steeped into view. The black leather plates of his armour seemed to merge into the darkness of the night, a pair of swords hung comfortably at his waist and his long black hair tied back giving Damitri a clear view of his face.

Damitri's eyes were drawn, however, to a figure he was dragging by the throat; from his garb he appeared to be a bowman. "You have done well, son of Decar, but this merry chase must now come to a close." The figure took several steps forward dragging the struggling bowman with him. "But first, my apologies about the cheek" he said as he raised a broken arrow, "it appears that when I say I need them intact and undamaged there seems to be some confusion on this." The figure suddenly raised the bowman off the ground easily with one hand while gesturing to the man with the other: "This is what an intact person looks like." Without another word he quickly hammered the broken arrow into the dangling figure's skull crushed the noise of which echoed within the now still forest. "And this is what a damaged person looks like. Do I need to demonstrate on someone else or do you all understand now?" The figure waited a moment before taking another step forward: "Good, so now we have that cleared up we can continue," his eyes falling on Selina before settling on Damitri. "Hello Damitri, it's been a while."

"Davaldion," was Damitri's single response.

After a brief moment passed Davaldion broke the silence again. "Give me the girl and out of respect for the man your father was, you can go." Without hesitating Damitri took a step forward. "You will not be having her," his voice defiant as he drew his sword.

Davaldion stood still, a look of dissatisfaction upon his face that quickly changed to one of amusement. "Very well, you may both leave, but on one condition." The malice in his voice was not lost on Damitri.

"And what is your condition?"

Davaldion smiled and drew the sword that hung to his left. "It's simple really; just beat me in a duel and you can walk free." With those words Damitri knew that he was truly trapped as before him stood Davaldion Du'Laraine, a swordsman whose skill demanded the respect of even the great elven blade dancers. Yet regardless of this, Selina's only hope lay with him beating a legend.

"Very well," Damitri replied as he released Selina's hand. "Fear not, M'lady," he said as he looked into her frightened eyes, "this is not where my story ends".

Turning back to his foe Damitri took a defensive stance.

"Shall we?" Davaldion smiled.

Selina closed her eyes and prayed for the man she had despised and hated for doing the task that had been given to him, a task to keep her safe, a task that had now pitted him against an unbeaten foe. She prayed he would win and that she could be safe again.

Selina heard the clash of steel and opened her eyes.

Chapter 4

Damitri stirred within his damp cell as the full realisation of his failure returned to him; for all his skill and training he lacked the ability to beat the likes of a thousand year old swords master. He tried to move and found himself chained to the wall.

"Selina," he called out desperately as the finality of the situation dawned on him.

"I'm here," she said from a dark corner of the cell. Unlike Damitri she had been placed within the cell untouched albeit chained to the wall..

"Are you ok?" His voice was dry and his face and ribs hurt. "I'm fine," she replied, "it's as though they're scared to touch me." A confused look was plain on her face, though Damitri knew why Davaldion's men feared her and he knew this was key to how he would find a way for them to escape.

A noise from the lock brought their attention to the doorway, and the imposing figure of Davaldion entered the chamber.

"Ah, you're awake," his gloating tone fuelling Damitri's anger at the situation he found himself in. "I would have hated for you to have slept through the sacrifice of something so delicate."

His words cut Selina deepest and tears quickly formed in her eyes. "Damn you, Davaldion, I will see you die for this!" Damitri roared his anger, blocking out the pain that ran through his body as he strained against his chains.

"Be quiet, half breed," came Davaldion's response as he punched Damitri, knocking him back against the wall. "You are alive at my bidding and I would be mindful of that fact."

"Which brings me to you." The cold stare of Davaldion fell upon the trembling girl that sat chained to the wall. "You are an agent of superstition and, if I may say so, a needless waste of my time." He suddenly flew at her, grabbing her by the throat and lifting her from the ground. "Tell me girl, why is it that powers greater than myself fear you?"

"I don't know," she sobbed.

"Tell me!" he shouted at her, "what power do you have over them?" his grip tightening.

The world darkened for Selina, but as she was about to give up she felt warmth within herself; a glow of hope that seemed to spread across her whole body, a warmth that settled within a single tear that ran down her cheek and landed on Davaldion's wrist.

Davaldion felt the magic immediately as a white fire burst from his hand, causing him to drop the girl to the ground. The burning pain from the flames intensified as they spread across his body making him cry out in anguish. "What did you do to me, you bitch!" he yelled at her, but Selina was unconscious on the ground. His mind was on fire and he staggered out of the chamber into the tunnels beyond.

Damitri looked at Selina's still figure and upon seeing her draw breath he relaxed, "so you have finally awoken, morning star," he mused to himself.

Deep below his prison a lone figure staggered the corridors; agony wracking his body as he fell into an empty chamber where his body collapsed to the floor. Davaldion felt the darkness around him, the void of the abyss opening below him as his master called another of its agents home. "And so it's oblivion," he thought as the blackness engulfed him. Just as the last of the light had left his vision, a single star of light appeared and with that, the darkness that had invaded the soul of Davaldion was gone.

Selina found herself very much alive when she regained consciousness. "Welcome back," Damitri quipped.

"What happened?" she asked.

"I don't know exactly what you did, only that you protected yourself," Damitri's solemnly replied.

"But that's impossible I don't know magic," she said, a defiant tone in her voice.

"No, you just didn't know you could use magic," Damitri sighed. "The fact you have this power is the reason I was given to you as a guardian and why we were heading to see Vermillion." He shuffled against his chains: "If anything, the fact you are able to manifest anything is a good sign that we may be able to get out of here. I'm just hoping the spectacle you made of Davaldion will buy us enough time to come up with something."

Davaldion's body awoke suddenly as he took his first breath in what appeared to have been an age. The realisation of what had come to pass fell upon him: the deaths he had dealt and innocents that he had corrupted. He wished it was only an age-old nightmare from which he had awoken but he knew it was true. A throbbing in his hand drew his attention to a burn scar; within it, a small crystal sat embedded in his hand and as he pulled it free, he remembered the white star and the words it had told him. "The girl," he whispered as he clambered to his feet and headed back towards the prison chamber.

Damitri watched from a helpless position as two more of the corrupted mercenaries poked and threatened Selina, gingerly trying to unchain her without getting too close. He knew he could try and break free of the chains but would they kill her before he had the chance to stop them?

As they finally removed her chains and Damitri considered making his move, the shadow in the centre of the chamber seemed to shift as it took the form of a single figure; a figure whose two swords rang out in unison, cutting the guards heads from their shoulders; a figure that both Damitri and Selina recognised. "Davaldion?"

"Listen to me carefully," Davaldion whispered, "they are waiting for her and more will come looking for her soon." When Damitri went to object Davaldion waved him down. "You have no reason to believe me as mere hours ago I would have seen you all dead," he quickly turned to Selina "but you did something to me that removed his hold over me, for when I awoke I had this." Slowly Davaldion produced the small crystal from his pocket.

"It can't be," Damitri said, a look of awe upon his face, "a soul stone; no one has seen one of these for over a hundred years."

"Indeed," Davaldion replied, turning back to Damitri "and he will know it's gone, which is why we must get you out of here now."

"And how do you expect us to trust you, regardless of what you say?"

Davaldion paused for a moment. "Look at it this way, you have one of two options: wait here and die because they will come back for her or take a chance that I am telling the truth and at least have a fighting chance of getting out of here," his tone now carrying a greater sense of urgency.

"Then I guess we have no choice other than to trust you," came Damitri's dejected reply.

"No, I guess you don't," Davaldion responded as he cut Damitri's chains and handed him his sword belt. "You will need this; I'm not expecting this to be a walk in the woods."

Davaldion turned to help to Selina to her feet and as she shifted away from him, he said "I know why you fear me and there is little I can do to change what I did to you, but I can use whatever time I have to make amends for what I have done." He knelt down before her and showed her the burns on his hands. "The world makes a point of offering second chances sparingly and I do not intend to waste mine, therefore I swear you will see the light of day before this day is through." It was with these words that Davaldion showed her the crystal and, as he did so it glowed with a perfect bright light. "Even the gods cannot make a soul stone lie," he whispered as he offered his hand. "Please M'lady, we need to go." Selina glanced at Damitri who nodded and she slowly took his hand.

"This way and keep close, they have all been drawn for the sacrificial meeting so for the most part the tunnels should be clear."

"Where are we?" Damitri asked.

"Deep below the forest," Davaldion replied without looking.

"Does the hive spread this far?"

"You would be surprised what festers beneath the world," came Davaldions response.

With the guidance of Davaldion they were able to quickly move into an outer tunnel where they found themselves moving away from the main concentration of chambers and Damitri began to feel a little more comfortable, even if he still didn't trust their benefactor.

"Wait here a moment," Davaldion said suddenly, "I need to slow them down." He quickly drew one of his swords and cut a support holding a segment of the ceiling in place causing it to collapse, blocking the tunnel behind them.

"How much longer?" Damitri questioned.

"An hour if we're lucky, it depends on how long it will take for them to get through this," he reply.

"Then we'd better keep moving," Damitri said as he offered Selina his hand.

They had not been traveling long when they heard the sound of movement beyond their makeshift barricade. "We don't have much time." Again Davaldion cut the supports of the tunnel which collapsed behind them. "There is only one more junction like this before we get to the surface." As the words left Davaldion's mouth the tunnels shook as the pursuing minions broke through the first barricade.

They ran, ran as fast as they could, until in the distance they could see the faint glimmer of daylight through the tunnel opening, but behind them they heard the second barricade buckle under the weight of their foes.

"You won't have time to reach the exit before they are upon us and this barricade won't hold them long enough," came the defeated response from Davaldion.

"We have to try," cried Damitri.

Davaldion slowed to a walk: "This is the last of the interchanges," he said turning to Selina. "M'lady, I wronged you. I said

I would make amends and that is something that I still wish to see fulfilled so I give to you three gifts." Again he produced the crystal soul stone and, taking her hand he placed the stone on her palm. "I give to you the freedom that you returned to me: keep it close and may it always remind you that even those that have strayed the furthest from the path may find it again someday."

"My second gift to you is this," he turned to Damitri and offered him a leather bundle, "this was my greatest possession from an age ago, it is hers now."

Letting go of her hand he took several steps backwards. "It's ironic, don't you think that I would walk the same path of your father so closely," he laughed at Damitri. "Get her to safety Damitri, get her into the light."

"You can't seriously be thinking of staying behind, they will tear you apart." Selina pleaded. "M'lady I have lived more in the last hour than I have in the last thousand years, which reminds me… "

His sword shone cutting the supporting beam, causing the tunnel to buckle as it began to collapse. "For my third gift I give you the gift of time, the time to get out of here and a moment of reflection for when you need it most, use them wisely. "

"No!" she cried, "we can all escape!"

"Goodbye M'lady" and with that the tunnel fell between them and he was gone.

Davaldion listened to her muffled cries as Damitri led her away.

"So, this is how it ends," he laughed to himself in the dark.

Drawing his swords he stood there alone in the corridor, closed his eyes and cleared his mind. Using the foul magic that he had mastered over the centuries he listened for the ripples in the air for the shadow walkers; he knew they would be coming first for they would be unseen by most, but not undetected by him.

It was a delicate vibration in the air at first but soon he could feel them coming and just as they were closing in on him, he struck.

His blades spun like a baton in the hands of a conductor as he played through his dark symphony of death, each telling blow revealing the location of the next. It was mere moments that had past but for those who had fallen upon his blades it was an eternity as they fell from the shadow plane back into view, their bodies covering the floor.

"I would suggest the rest of you face me head on," he called out into the shadows.

And as if the darkness heard him they moved before him until the host of Ragnor stood before him.

"You are a fool to betray us, Davaldion," a heavy set axe-wielding bandit called forth.

"Then please come and punish me," he retorted.

The bandit was cowed by the challenge and Davaldion laughed.

"What is the meaning of this, Davaldion?" a deep voice cried out as the large muscular figure of Ragnor came into view, his large glave held firmly in his hand.

"What can I say, I had a change of heart and decided to work for the other side," came Davaldion's flippant response.

Ragnor's tone grew deadly. "You will die slowly for what you have done"

"Will that be from the conversation or do you have something more interesting planned?"

"Enough! Kill him!" Ragnor roared.

But enough was the reputation of Davaldion that none dared step forward to meet his blades.

"You cowards." Ragnor brought his glaive to bear on the nearest bandit, rending him in two. "Kill him."

"To the death," Davaldion told himself as the bandits and mercenaries charged.

Again the twin blades of Davaldion swung free and the first five of his assailants fell immediately and, though they were quickly replaced, the following fighters were not so sure of their numbers. A sixth fell quickly followed by a seventh and an eighth. Throats were cut, limbs were severed, bodies were impaled and still he carried on.

"I am death incarnate!" Davaldion roared as his blades swung round, beheading another target, "is there no one among you up to the task of ending me?"

Ragnor suddenly leapt into the fray, his glaive spinning in a cruel arc cutting down one of his own men. Davaldion's blades clashed with the glaive and for the first time Davaldion found himself being forced to retreat.

But Davaldion was not so easily defeated. He quickly changed his footing and after weaving past Ragnor's next blow he moved to his side, striking a quick glancing blow against the giant man's shoulder, who quickly reversed a sweeping blow behind him. But Davaldion was already moving to attack his intended target and his blades quickly cut through Ragnor's tendons causing him to fall to his knees.

Leaving him the opportunity he needed to finish his foe, Davldion moved to finish the fallen Ragnor. But as he did so the very shadows seemed to rise up against him, and Davaldion knew that his time was over, for the darkness looks after its own and Davaldion had turned his back on his previous master.

"You backed the wrong side, Davaldion," Ragnor gloated from the floor as tendrils of darkness burst from the shadows, impaling Davaldion and lifting him from the ground.

Blood flew from his mouth as he felt the all familiar cold of the dark entering his body, but Davaldion had one last act of defiance. With the last of his strength he threw his sword at the gloating Ragnor where it impaled him through the mouth.

His defiance, however, cost him dearly, and he found himself crashing to the ground as the tendrils moved around his limbs and pulled his body tight.

"You were wrong to step back into the light, Davaldion," the disembodied voice called, "the followers of light will only find death within this world."

"On the contrary," Davaldion grimaced, "I will be waiting at the gates for what's left of you once she's finished with you and then we will see what's waiting for us beyond this world."

"We shall see," and with that the tendrils of darkness tore the body of Davaldion apart.

Damitri finally found himself at the entrance of the tunnel and let out a sigh of relief as he felt the sun on his face. Turning to Selina he smiled, "he really did come through for us."

"I know," she replied as she watched the soul stone she carried glow one last time.

Chapter 5

The sky grew dark from the approaching evening as the grey stone walls of Reul Na Maidne finally came into view. Damitri afforded himself the luxury of a sigh of relief. "Come on" he said, leading Selina by the hand, "we need to get inside by nightfall." As he led her down the road he knew that the sun would keep the fiends that hunted them at bay, but they would arrive in force at nightfall.

Galewyn watched Damitri approach from his balcony and let out a sigh of relief. "At least that is one of the daughters accounted for," he sighed as he made his way back into his chamber. Moving over to the oak wardrobe he produced his priestly robes of Shi'Ara. "Best I look the part," he chuckled to himself.

Selina noticed Damitri's entire demeanour change as soon as they entered the grounds of the ancient temple as though, he had been carrying a great burden which had been lifted from his shoulders. She was also tired and exhausted from her encounter in the tunnels beneath the forest the previous night, and when a seat was offered she quickly accepted.

"I need to speak with the master of chantry about last night, I will return in a while," Damitri said as she seated herself. He pointed to a middle aged monk who stood to the side of the room. "Brother Galen will take you to a room where you can eat and rest and we can talk later, I promise," and with that he left through a large pair of oak double doors.

With his departure Selina felt herself suddenly overcome with a feeling of isolation and, as she nervously looked around the dining hall, her eyes fell upon the monk who smiled gently at her. "Do not worry Madainn Reul, you are quite safe." He unfolded his arms and gestured towards the doorway: "Come, you must be tired from your journey, there will be time for answers later." Selina smiled back and after slowly rising to her feet she realised he he was right, she did have questions, but she was exhausted and the chance of sleep sounded appealing. "What was that you called me?" she asked as he led her to her room." "It's simply a term of reverence, M'Lady," he smiled as he opened the door to her chamber. "If you need me, I will be outside your room," and with that he left her alone.

Selina awoke to a tapping on her door and as she opened her eyes she found a single candle glowing in the corner of her room. The narrow window in her room showed the nights sky and she groaned as she climbed up from her bed, the aches and pains from her previous night's ordeal finally beginning to take their toll.

The knock came from the door again. "I'm coming," she called out as she stumbled over to the door. She lifted the bolt and opened it to be greeted by the familiar face of Damitri.

"I'm sorry to have woken you," he apologised, "but I have someone who wishes to speak with you." She nodded and, after using the basin to wake herself, she followed Damitri down the hall until they stopped at a large ornate door.

"Please be patient," Damitri said turning to her, "we will answer all your questions before the night is through," and with that Damitri knocked once and opened the door.

The interior of the room was obviously used by a sage or other learned man as ancient tomes and scrolls littered the shelves and walls of the room.

A large tapestry ran along the wall and showed what seemed to be a climactic battle, and from the archaic writing Selina believed to have been in ancient times as the tapestry itself showed the wear and stains of time.

"Please take a seat," a voice rang out and she found her attention drawn to a robed figure stood in front of the window, the afternoon sun hiding his features from her.

Damitri moved over to a seat and offered it to her. She gave Damitri an apprehensive look before sitting down"I expect you have a great many questions Selina, daughter of Sofia," the figure continued without moving. "Wait, you know of my mother?" Selina found the simple statement rocking through her and she almost found herself standing.

"Indeed," the figure said turning back to her, revealing his kind features, "I have heard a great deal about you, Madainn Reul"

She shot a glance to Damitri a confused look her face. "But first," the figure stated loudly, "let me introduce myself." His voice seemed to soften as he moved from the window to stand next to her.

He held his hand out to her and when she offered him hers he took it gently in his aged hands and cupped it almost reverently. "My name is Galewyn and I am the head of this chantry," he continued. "Damitri has brought you here for your safety and, more importantly, answers." He released her hand and sat behind a large desk piled with scrolls and pieces of parchment. Her eyes were drawn to a large tome that was open on the desk in front of him.

He paused for a moment as if considering his next words carefully. "Tell me of the events of last night," he said suddenly. The directness of his question caught Selina off guard and she found herself reliving the events of the night before. The sacrifice of Davaldion came to the forefront of her mind again and she found herself reaching for the stone that he passed her the last time as she recited her ordeal.

After waiting a moment for a teary Selina to compose herself, Galewyn continued: "I think it would be most prudent to start at the beginning."

"At the dawn of things there was the void and endless vastness of time and space, an arena of infinite possibilities and potential. There was no light or darkness, nor was their time or space.

"For the void existed within a single instance, a single gap between moments and time. "Yet it is said that within this moment in time there existed a

being of unimaginable power, a being whose power rivalled even that of the gods; however, the existence of this being is known only to a few and to these few he is known as the Sleeper.

"No one knows how the Sleeper came to be within the void, nor do we know why he sleeps; we do, however, know that he dreams. "For it was the Sleeper's dream taking form that created our world and the very stars in the sky.

"Though at times the Sleeper's dreams turned dark, and with that the elder gods came into being: they were greedy and spiteful and vied for dominion over all things.

"With little regard for the creatures and races that were caught in their plots, the creations of the Sleeper had become pawns in a game they could not comprehend.

"Millennia passed and so vast was the destruction and slaughter of the dark god wars, that as ancient plots unfolded on the elder peoples of Ollundra their screams for aid were heard beyond the world of Ollundra and, for the first in the history of the world, the Sleeper stirred.

"What began as a simple stirring of his sleep became a single waking moment and the Sleeper saw all that he had created and all that the elder gods had done.

"In that very moment the Phadrea came into being and the great divine war began, as the Sleeper returned to his slumber.

"The divine war ended as suddenly as it had begun, with the majority of the elder gods slain or imprisoned eternally in the shadows of the world, yet such was the destruction of the war that it was decreed that no god would again interfere with the mortal world.

"Yet, for even though the Phadrea had been victorious their victory was not complete, for one of the greatest of their number had remained hidden and from its hiding place it watched the world unfold and flourish while it bided its time.

"It was a thousand years later that the last of the elder gods flung himself onto the mortal plane and sundered the world, corrupting and changing the world as it passed and the Phadrea could do nothing but watch in horror, for the lord of the Phadrea enforced their covenant.

"Yet Shi'Ara, the lady of light, rebelled and bestowed a great power in a mortal princess or a northern empire of me, a power that created an order of dawn maidens, the Madainn Reul.

"The war of the darkness and light ended when the last of the elder gods was shattered across the world and with the passing of the first of the dawn maidens, though her daughters carried on the sisterhood, a sisterhood that exists to this very day.

Galewyn closed the book as he finished. "The reason you are being hunted, my dear lady, is due to the fact they suspect your lineage," he glanced at Damitri, "and from what I understand from the events of last night, their assumptions were true."

"Wait," Selina interrupted, "you're telling me that I went through hell last night because of something that happened a thousand years ago?" Her anger boiled within her as she growled "Where was my choice in this?" she stood up and turned to leave.

"Selina," Galewyn said, his voice now carrying a tone of authority causing her to stop. "Regardless of your thoughts of the legitimacy of heritage, the danger you are in is all too real."

She turned back to him, tears in her eyes. "But why me" she pleaded, "all I ever wanted was to be married and cared for by a husband."

A glance from Galewyn gave Damitri his cue and he moved to stand beside her. "They hunt you because they fear what you will become." Reaching to her clenched hand Damitri turned it and gently opened her fist revealing a crystal. "Davaldion gave his life to protect you because he understood your importance"

Damitri gestured back towards her chair. "Please, listen to what he has to say, I promise I will not let any harm to come to you." The look in his eyes made her soften and though she couldn't understand why, she reluctantly returned to her seat and Galewyn continued.

"I need you to understand, today has only been a reprieve." Galewyn sat down, his hands face down upon the table. "This chantry was built centuries ago as a place of refuge against the minions of the fallen, but tonight, despite our best efforts and our defences, they will come for you with everything they can muster." Seeing the look of fear crossing her face Galewyn smiled. "I promise this to you, that you will see the morning come." He suddenly looked towards the door. "Galen," he called suddenly. The door opened as Brother Galen quietly entered the chamber.

"Galen, Selina is in need of a guardian as we are expecting unwelcome guests tonight. Are you up to the task?" Damitri looked betrayed and though to Selina Galewyn's words were phrased as a question he knew that it was nothing more than a concealed order.

The monk quietly bowed. "I understand, I will let no harm come to her," he reverently replied. "Thank you Galen, she will join you shortly." The monk bowed again and left the chamber as Galewyn brought his attention to a shocked Damitri "You will be needed elsewhere, Galen will be more than capable of protecting her." The finality of his words caused Damitri's face to darken and he lowered his head.

"I think it would be an idea for you to get prepared Selina, it's going to be a very long night." He motioned to the door: "Galen will arrange everything for you."

Surprised by the sudden dismissal, she stood and turned to head towards the door when she stopped and turned towards him.

"May I ask you a question?" she asked. "Anything you wish, Madainn Reul" he nodded. "What does Madainn Reul mean? Several people have called me this since I arrived." Galewyn smiled. "It's an ancient term that goes back to the first war of Shadow. It roughly translates into the Imperial tongue as Morning Star, for the light of the daughters of Shi'Ara gifted the world with a new dawn." Selina was stunned by his answer; Galewyn continued: "There are people here that believe in you Selina, even if you doubt your role yourself." She nodded quietly and left the chamber.

"Why wouldn't you want me by her side?" Damitri started as soon as the door was closed. "They will send everything they have Damitri, I cannot spare you to sit at the heart of the chantry when you could be of far more use at our defences." Damitri began to argue but Galewyn continued: "And I would fathom that there are some who would happily seek you out in order to further their own ends." Shaking his head Damitri sighed, "So I'm to be bait." For all he detested Galewyn's orders, in his heart Damitri knew that Galewyn was right. "As you wish," he solemnly replied.

Selina was joined by Galen as she left Galewyn's and stormed towards her room. She was angry and frightened, she missed the luxuries and the feeling of safety of her home and most of all she doubted what she had been told. Yet what frustrated her most was that after her meeting with Davaldion she couldn't help but feel that maybe Galewyn was right.

She stopped suddenly and looked behind herself where ten steps behind her stood Galen, his head bowed. "You don't need to follow me," she said sharply, her hands moving to her hips "it's not nightfall yet." "M'Lady, you are my ward and I will be at your side until someone replaces me or someone removes me against my choosing," came his softly spoken reply.

Stunned by the sincerity of his reply Selina felt her hands drop from her hips. "Look at me, Galen," her tone now gentle, his soft blue eyes raised to meet hers. "Do you really believe that I am this grand saviour?" Galen simply smiled.

"There has yet to be a time when the master of the chantry has been wrong, but the enemy believes you are what they say you are and as such they will come for you." He took a further step towards her. "But the master has asked for you to be guarded and regardless of you being the one they seek or not, we will defend you to the end."

"The end?" she asked, "what end?" her words shaking as her anger left her and with the realisation of the magnitude of the coming night, she knew the answer before he replied: "Everyone within this chantry has taken an oath to stand before the darkness no matter the cost, you will see another dawn, M'Lady."

Gesturing again for her to continue walking, he said, "I would suggest you get something to eat and some sleep, we are expecting a very long night." Selina nodded softly and headed down the corridor, Galen following ten steps behind her.

Selina awoke with a start and found herself lying alone within a forest clearing. As she climbed to her feet she found herself adorned in a golden gown of gossamer silk, the sun was shining above her and the grass was gentle beneath her bare feet.

"Hello?" she called.

"Remember this place Madainn Reul, for it is my gift to you, a place between moments where you may rest," a voice called out, the voice was definitely female but had an otherworldly ring to it.

Selina became aware that there was somebody else behind her but as she turned she found herself waking in her room in the chantry, Galen stood next to her. "M'Lady, it is time," he calmly stated as he offered her his hand.

As she climbed to her feet he offered his hand forward and as he opened it she found Davaldion's soul stone mounted on a silver chain. "I apologise for any offence this may have caused but I thought this would make it easier to carry." Selina smiled as she took the chain from his hand and put it around her neck.

"Thank you," she smiled.

As they left her room she saw that the calm monks and guards she had seen earlier were now brandishing heavy arms and armour and people rushed to their positions. "Where are we going?" she asked as he led her down the corridor.

"To the heart of the chantry," Galen simply replied as he led her down the chambers and stairways until they eventually came to a large iron door adorned with silver runes.

Galen opened the door and politely gestured for her to enter when a voice called out. Turning, Selina saw the slender figure of Damitri descending the stars. Damitri gave a quick nod to Galen as he passed Selina a leather bound bundle: "Here, I hope you will never need to use it," he said.

"What is it?" she asked

"A parting gift from a friend," he replied as he turned and headed back up the stairs. "Take care of her Galen," he called back as Galen closed the door between them.

The inside of the chamber was adorned with more of the silver runes and several tapestries hung neatly upon the walls. Several benches were placed around the edges of the room with a shrine to Shi'Ara standing as a centre piece.

Taking one of the seats Selina watched as Galen knelt before the shrine and closed his eyes. Gently she began to unwind the leather package that Damitri had given her, tears coming to her eyes as she revealed the jewelled blade of Davaldion. "Fear not M'Lady, Shi'Ara will not desert us." Galen's voice was an echo of calm and she felt herself relax in her seat.

Chapter 6

Damitri returned to his post on the roof of the chantry where fifty other men readied themselves, their eyes on the setting sun as the last of the day's light disappeared behind the distant mountains.

Damitri slowly unsheathed his sword and looked at the blade, calming his mind ahead of what was to follow when he felt a comforting hand on his shoulder. "Easy lad," a familiar voice said as he looked up to see large bearlike figure of Wulfren looking at him.

"You didn't think that I wouldn't be willing to help you?" he said with a smile, Damitri allowed himself an answering smile as he glanced at the hulking fighter dressed in his silvered steel armour and carrying his signature axe.

"That armour looks a little tight, maybe you should lay off the ale," Damitri joked as they shared a moment of respite before the coming night.

A shout from the lookout above them warned them that the first of the attackers had come into view, and what was going to be a long night began.

Far beyond the guarded rooftop of the chantry, the shadows of the land before them stirred as the foul creatures and minions of the fallen crawled from their hiding places and descended upon the tower.

Where at first there were a few, their numbers swelled as a swarm of the Fallen's minions swarmed upon the lone tower, the defending archers punishing the over eager darklings that moved towards the tower.

"Shall we get started?" Wulfren quipped with a wide grin as he moved towards the nearest wall.

"Sometimes you really scare me," Damitri mumbled as he followed.

From his window Galewyn watched the oncoming horde and silently reached for his staff. After taking a moment to focus himself, he placed his staff on a single silver rune upon his floor and let the power of Shi'Ara flow through him as he called out into the night: "May the light of Shi'Ara be the beacon of hope in places where only the shadows lie."

A blast of radiant light emanated from his staff as the rune began to glow, the pulsing light leapt to thousands of other runes littered around the tower that sprung into life, emitting a radiant silver light that quickly engulfed the tower.

Selina was surprised by the sudden glow of the runes as they lit up around the chamber, her head snapped across to where Galen was kneeling. "They are here," came his simple reply.

Atop the chantry the sudden burst of light erupting from the tower had slowed the initial assault as the weaker minions of the Fallen found themselves reduced to ash in an instant, with those that survived quickly burrowing themselves back under ground in order to escape the glowing light.

"Ready yourselves," Damitri cried out to the sentries atop the chantry as the first of the shadowkin ascended the walls of the tower with unnatural grace landing amongst the waiting defenders, their faces and skin blackened by the radiant light around them.

An axe wielding fiend landed to Damitri's right and quickly lashed out with its great weapon. Damitri ducked to one side as he let the blow pass him as he became aware of a second attacker to his rear. Grabbing the overextended blow of the fiend, Damitri dragged him forward and off balance as he moved to face a towering wolf headed monstrosity that thrust a clawed towards him. Damitri reacted when the beast arched its back and fell to the ground, a large silver axe buried in its back. Wulfren roared in triumph as pulled his axe free and beheaded a small impish looking creature that had leapt over the wall.

Damitri turned his attention back to the fallen fiend and despatched it as it tried to regain its footing. Three sword wielding shadow weavers descended upon him, their dual blades spinning as they moved using their affinity with the shadow plane to flit into and out of view as they attacked, their superior numbers and abilities ensuring them a swift kill on the single defender.

Damitri recognised their style as a crude form of Davaldion's own fighting technique, which gave him a quick insight into their ability and his first advantage. His second advantage came from his father's taint and Damitri flittered from view, to the surprise of his attackers who found themselves fighting a swordsman instantaneously on the mortal and shadow planes.

Their blows were fast and Damitri found himself deflecting seven instantaneous blows, his blade a blur hidden amongst his attackers' blows, and just as his attackers seemed to gain the upper hand, Damitri struck.

His sword reversed in a fraction of a second and slid between the defences of the first of his attackers, slicing them open across their abdomen, the loss of momentum showing on their faces as they found their attacks turned against them. Damitri beheaded the second and impaled the third before reappearing on the mortal plane and turning his focus to his next target.

A mile away from the Chantry, on a hill, several figures stood watching the fighting unfold. Ahead of them stood a large figure, a purple flame burned in his eyes. "Menlock, get the girl," his icy tone dripping with malice. To his side a large figure climbed from the depths of the figure's own shadow, slowly unfolding until it unravelled into a towering winged monstrosity of horns, claws and fangs.

"As you wish" it roared as it took to the sky.

Wulfren saw the descending shape as it headed towards the tower and realised that the rooftop was not its goal. "In Shi'Ara's name," he mumbled as he turned and shouted a warning to the struggling defenders as the hulking mass of the demon crashed against the stone walls of the chantry, smashing the runes and leaving a hole in the wall of the tower.

"He's going for the girl!" Wulfren shouted to Damitri "go, we'll handle this" and without a word Damitri turned and headed to the stairway down.

At the heart of the chantry Galen looked up as he felt the room shake, his hand moving to the holy symbol of Shi'Ara that hung from his neck.

The cracking of stone drew his attention to the wall near Selina and he shot to his feet; grabbing her, he pulled her to the ground as the wall of the chamber cracked open and a black tendril of shadow punched through the wall, lashing towards Selina who screamed in fright.

Yet Galen was there, his leg quickly arching in to a circular kick, striking the tendril and in a burst of light the tendril turned to ash. "Stay behind me," he said, his voice keeping his usual calm tone.

Two shadow kin quickly jumped through the ruptured wall and with their rusted blades in hands, they charged the unarmed monk, the first leading with a crude overhand strike. Selina's mouth opened as Galen hardly seemed to move, yet his attacker flew harmlessly over his shoulder only to find Galen's foot snap down upon his neck. Undeterred by the monk's actions, the second shadow kin moved to attack, only to feel the monk grip on his arm as Galen redirected the attacker's momentum and flipped the shadow kin, its head rolling down its own blade beheading itself with the weapon it still held in its hand.

His head snapped towards where Selina was laying and he grabbed her hand and pulled her towards him as a shadow weaver shot into view. Galen spun Selina behind him his foot kicking the shadow weaver's hand and knocking the blade from its grip before spinning and kicking it in the face knocking it back to the floor.

Removing his sash from around his waist he took a step back to Selina. "Quick! Get to the doorway." The need for haste was evident in his tone as another shadow weaver appeared next to Selina only to find Galen's sash wrapped around its neck, which promptly broke under the monk's skilful hands.

The chamber wall gave way as the demon moved to enter the chamber, black tendrils of shadow stretching from its outstretched hand that Galen moved to disperse, but the demon had only intended to distract the monk as several shadow weavers appeared next to Selina, their blades falling down upon her.

Galen, becoming aware of the ploy, snapped the holy symbol from around his neck and slammed it into the demon's brow. The demon roared in agony as it staggered back, clawing at the symbol as it burnt into its skull. The shadow weavers fell towards the terrified girl who crudely brought Davaldion's sword before her, causing her attackers to laugh.

A laughter that was cut short as Galen stuck, his blows were fast and precise and the weavers found themselves fleeing to the shadow realm, but Galen was a monk of Shi'Ara and his hands reached beyond the mortal realm, dragging them back into the chantry as he broke them apart with his bare hands.

Turning to check on Selina, the monk was relieved to see that she was uninjured, her eyes suddenly going wide as she screamed a warning, a warning that was given too late. Galen felt the agony of the blow as the spear like shaft of shadow impaled him, lifting him from his feet as the hulking demon came back into view, a silver scar now adorning its brow.

"Run!" Galen cried to Selina as the demon threw the dying monk to the ground and charged towards the shaking girl, a large sword of shadow forming in its hands that it brought down upon her.

Selina surprised herself as she raised her sword to block, yet such was the weight of the blow it knocked her from her feet and she found herself falling backwards, screaming in terror as she fell.

Selina felt herself hit the ground but did not find herself on the floor of the chamber; she found herself in the same forest grove from her dream and she scrambled to feet, sword in hand.

"Am I dead?" she asked out loud.

"No," replied a male voice, and as she spun her she staggered back her eyes wide with shock.

"Davaldion," her voice was full of shock, "I thought you were dead."

He smiled. "well part of me is." He took a step forward "I gave you the major part of my being in the tunnels, that part of me is now bound to you." He turned around in the clearing. "This is a place of refuge for you. I've been here ever since my body died." He turned to her again. "You're in a pocket of time, whisked away from all that surrounds you and, from what I guess, things aren't looking too good for you."

"There are too many of them and I can't fight them," she whimpered as she began to sob.

She didn't notice Davaldion move behind her until he reached around her and took her hands. "Alas my lady I am no longer able to fight for you." He gently moved her hands as she looked around at him. "I can, however guide you."

"What?" her confusion evident.

"I'm saying that I can guide the sword in your hands, if you will let me."

He moved her arm and she felt the blades weight . "If you are to remember anything from this visit, remember this: you will never need to feel alone again"

The world spun around her and Selina found herself back in the chamber staring into the burnt face of her attacker, her sword perfectly placed in front of her to block his incoming blow.

Before she knew it the blade flipped in her hands, causing her foe to fall forward as she stepped sideways. Her arm was already coming down in an arc, the blade smoothly cutting down her attacker.

"Move," she heard Davaldion say as she felt herself moved forward, as though pushed, her sword arm again moving to deflect the myriad of oncoming blows that her enemies rained down upon her before calmly cutting them down with ease.

Surprised by her display, the demon found the girl moving on the offensive as it fought her to keep her salvo of blows at bay. Seizing an opportunity it slashed at her and Selina found herself moving straight towards it. This move shocked it as she sidestepped its blow and impaled the demon through its abdomen, causing it to roar out in anguish.

Before she had time to move the demon grabbed her: "I will tear you apart, Bitch!"

Selina cried out in pain as the demon pulled her arms apart, she heard Galen scream her name as he struggled to stand. "Now would be a good time to remember" she heard Davaldion say, his words ringing in her ears. "Wake up Madainn Reul," he shouted. The name shook her and she felt the familiar heat within: her eyes glowed silver and the demons gripped loosened. "What are you?" it cried in shock as the glow from her eyes spread to the whole of her body.

"I am the beacon in the darkness" she spoke in a now unearthly voice "and this girl is not yours to take."

The demon dropped Selina as the light from her body began to burn it. "May oblivion take you!" she roared as a wave of silver light burst from her body, sending silver light in a column from the depths of the tower to the sky above, reducing all the tainted in its path to ash.

From his view point upon the hillside the figures watched their army quickly reduced to ash. "So she has awoken," the shadowy figure said, "and so the circle begins anew," and with that he quietly turned and disappeared back into the shadows.

As the light faded Selina found herself dropping to her knees as utter exhaustion rocked her body. She looked over to the fallen body of Galen, who gazed at her with the same kind eyes despite the pool of blood he sat in.

"To the end Madainn Reul," he whispered as his eyes closed for the final time. "Galen," she whispered as the last of her strength left her and she crumpled to the ground.

***

Selina awoke in her bed to find Damitri sat in a chair asleep. She moved and he looked up, smiling. "It's good to see you awake," he sighed in relief.

"Why?" she asked, "how long have I been asleep?"

"A couple of days" came the reply.

"What happened?" she asked as she sat up.

"Don't you recall? It appears that Galewyn was right about you." He stood up and moved to her bedside. "You did something that I have not seen done for an age; you cast a spell that purified the entire

Chantry." he knelt down "it must have really taken it out of you as I found you unconscious when the light died down."

"So what now?" she shrugged. "Now we take you to the temple of Shi'Ara in the capital and hopefully they can help you understand what happened last night."

"When do we leave?" she asked as she moved to get up. "As soon as you're well enough to travel," Damitri replied as he moved towards the doorway.

"Damitri" she called after him "What happened to Galen?" Damitri bowed his head: "I'm sorry but he didn't make it." He turned back to her. "He died fulfilling a duty that he gladly accepted. We're preparing the bodies of the brothers we lost for burial if you would like to say goodbye?"

"I would like that very much" she smiled.

The End

About the Author

Craig Teal is the owner of Composite Games and the creator of the Chronicles of Ollundra and Unseen World game setting. The Fall and Redemption of Davaldion will be Craig's second published story. With the Crown of Thorns being his first published story and the origin story behind the Unseen World.

Of Mice and Dragons

By

Mary Hukel

Chapter 1

I had always known I was destined for great things. A farm was just a way to waste my talents. The world was waiting for me to take flight and claim my rightful place.

But first, I had to leave.

My father had plans for me. Wanting a son, he had to settle for a daughter. Ever the optimist, he figured that he could at least marry me off to the first oaf that belonged to a neighboring farmer. Before I could let that happen, I had to do something. Anything, really, that didn't involve me being married to the next local stud to continue the existance of farmers pledged to the King.

In the middle of the night, I tiptoed across the floor to open the door and sneak out. As it shut behind me, I did a little dance for my light-footed-ness. It was short-lived, however, when I realized that I had left my pack beside my bed. Silently cursing, I attempted to open the door and sneak back in.

My father's hunting dog had other ideas.

As I pelted down the road at a flat run, I hastily made other plans about food and lodgings. Snares could trap food, and I could bed down in barns overnight. So long as the other farms didn't have hunting dogs.

Of course, the realization of all my hunting equipment being in my pack back home dawned on me as I panted at the crossroads. As the saying goes, the best-laid plans of mice and dragons often lead to cheese. I'm not sure exactly what that saying could possibly mean, because my grandfather uttered those words on his deathbed, but I'm sure it had nothing to do with the sudden burst of rain that began as I stood and cursed and kicked and eventually slipped in the mud to land flat on my back, letting my tears mingle with the rain...

■■■

"Excuse me?"

The tears had dried long ago as the rain had stopped, and the sun beat down mercilessly on my eyelids as I laid on my back, my body molded to the road by the mud. "Excuse me?" I'd been like that all night, willing myself to be eaten by the earth so as to avoid a humiliating return home. "Excuse me?" But as the sun rose I could only think that I should go home and try again. *If* I weren't married to the first available lout once I set foot in the door.

A shadow blocked out the sun. "Excuse me, but is this the road to Ironhill?" I cracked open one eye to regard the speaker. A girl my age had bent over me to ask for directions to the very city I needed to lose myself in. "Do you speak common? Oh, wait, you're wearing farming clothes. You must be one of the locals. I really should have used a slower speech pattern." She cleared her throat and began to sign as she spoke. "Do...you..know..."this" road..."

"...is the one that leads to Ironhill? That takes you away from the farms and the stink and hard winters? Well, I wouldn't know. Seeing that I am but "simple folk," I suppose that laying on a muddy road after a hard rain near a full moon would be a custom you're not familiar with, but, yes, the road to Ironhill is a favored spot for the slow-witted to spend a day wallowing in the mud. Good day." I laid my head back down and closed my eyes once more.

"Ah, well. Excuse me, then. I shall be on my way." The footsteps hurried off, and I felt the guilt creep in. I peeled myself from the road, omethin, "Wait!" and slogged to my feet. The figure turned slowly, a passive mask on her face. Her hair was bound in a scarf that hid most of it, framing her oval face. The clothing she wore seemed impractical for travel, being a plain white shift, but I figured that she must have her reasons. "I'm sorry. I didn't mean to be rude, but..." And it all tumbled out in a rush, from the fear of being married off to the failed plans of escape. She listened as we walked, allowing me to purge the feelings of doom that had been building up. "...and that's where you found me. I do apologize, but, it's, well, been one of those nights..."

"It certainly seems so," she replied. "I can see why you would leave; being married off to someone you don't know does seem an awful fate, but I think there are worse things in the world."

"Oh really?"

"Well, yes! Wounded in battle and unable to provide a living for yourself or your family. Or not even knowing your own name!"

I thought about that for a moment, then paused, stuck out my hand, and said, "By the way, my name's Maya, and I'm just starting out on the road to Ironhill. Who might you be?"

She firmly grasped my hand, smiling widely. "Well, Maya, I am Dah'nelle, Initiate to Fortuae Cosmina. Pleased to meet you."

"Fortuae Cosmina? The Goddess of Fortune and Luck?"

"The very same!" My face must have given something away, for her brow furrowed and she put her hands on her hips. "And what's wrong with being and Initiate of the Goddess of Fortune and Luck?"

"Oh, oh, nothing, really. I mean, if it weren't for luck, particularly bad, I'd have no luck a't'all...!"

"Maya, do you have no faith?"

"I have faith that we're still a long way from Ironhill." My stomach growled. "And that we'll probably starve on the way there..."

"Nonsense! I'm sure that we'll find something along the way."

"I'm sure that you're right, Dah'nelle. But just in case you're wrong, do you have anything we can eat, so that we can keep going? As I said before, I had to leave my home in rather great haste..."

"Well, I only packed enough for one, since I wasn't sure I'd be able to find a ride into Ironhill, but we'll share, and Fortunae Cosmina will provide as we continue." I only smiled and nodded as we sat upon the side of the road, and she shared her sparse provisions with me. Hard cheese with equally hard bread and extremely tart and under ripened apples sat like a lump in my gut. "Where did you get these apples?" I managed around a sour mouthful.

"They were on the side of the road near an orchard. There was a farmer's hand that yelled at me, but I said that since it was on my side of the fence and not his, then they were available to anyone who wanted them. He said some rather nasty things, but I just took them and walked away. Why?"

I coughed down the last bite of fruit before answering, "Oh, nothing....yet..." The unripened fruit was going to be merciless down the road, and after a swallow or three of water from her water skein, I stood up, stretched, and turned at the sound of wagon wheels. "Oh, hey, look, a wagon! I wonder where they are heading?"

Dah'nelle gathered her things and stood, shielding her eyes from the sun. "Well, only one way to find out." She stepped out onto the road and waved down the driver. He pulled up beside us, and eyed us warily. I let Dah'nelle do the talking, and after a moment or two, we were in the back of the wagon with the farmer's wares that he was taking as tithe to Ironhill. We grinned at one another as we bounced along the road, then she lifted her face to the sky and whispered, "Thank you, Cosmina!"

Chapter 2

At the gate some three days later, we made our way on foot into the city. Dah'nelle had given the farmer a secret blessing, marking some of his boxes with a piece of charcoal she had in her pack. As he drove away, I asked about the mark, and why she didn't let him know about it. "That's how Fortunae Cosmina works. She never asks for recognition. You give a blessing of luck to whomever without their knowledge, and it follows them for a while. The trick is knowing when to hold back on your luck."

"I'm not sure I follow."

"Let's say I gave you a blessing to win a game of chance. You win three cards out of the pile, and that gives you a bit of a win. But when you get greedy and bet for more, your luck could turn sour."

"I'm still not sure I follow." I held up a hand to stay any further explanations. "But that doesn't mean that it doesn't work. So I will simply accept your faith in this." I looked around the city, intimidated by the sheer size of it. "Where do we begin? Where will we stay?"

"Well, I could stay at the temple. Cosmina's temples usually have beds, as luck would have it."

"That's all good and well for you, but I have no place to go, really..."

"Izzat so?" The sound of the voice sent shivers up my spine, reminding me of when my father would tell us tales by the fire as the wind howled outside in winter. Turning slowly, I looked upon a man no taller than I, a stout beard on a broad face, stout in stature, and, quite frankly, just about everything about him was stout. Including his breath as he spoke again. "If'n yer lookin' fer someplace to spend th' night, Lassie, then ye'd be best headin' t'th' Oak'n Staff....I hear they'll give ye someplace t'rest yer head...."

"Oaken Staff? Where would that be?" It always pays to be polite, I was often told by my mother, who would be beside herself in shame if she knew I was ever rude to anyone.

"Aahhh...no' the Oak'n Staff, the Oak...N....Staff...."

"Isn't that what I said...?"

"I think he means the Oak and Staff, Maya. Thank you, good sir, for giving us the name of the establishment. Shall we say who sent us?"

"Th'name's Rhyben, Lassie. They'll know t'give ye lasses a warm welcome."

"Thanks," I mumbled, not sure if it was a good idea to follow the mutterings of a drunken dwarf, but I was more than happy that I would be able to find a warm bed. The back of the wagon was hard and the nights still held the coolness of spring despite the warm days coming. I'd managed to find a corner of tarp that covered the farmer's harvest to use as a blanket, but it couldn't come with me, now. We headed off down the road in the direction Rhyben pointed, and we wandered a moment before we had to admit that we were sort of lost.

"Well, of course we're sort of lost. We've never been here before," said Dah'nelle as we turned down another alley. "We're bound to do that once or twice while we're here. So let's just keep heading in this direction..." We turned about, deciding to backtrack when our way was blocked by three men. My guts clenched and my throat went dry, knowing what would come next. I forced my hands into fists to keep them from shaking as I concentrated on each face. I could hear Dah'nelle something beside me, seeking Cosmina's blessing and asking if she could lend us a hand. I held little hope for help as the men started towards us.

"Well, well, well. Got turned around, did we?" I narrowed my gaze at the speaker, realizing that something was off. Surely he was tall, but thin, as if he were an understuffed scarecrow. The timbre of his voice was off, as well, as if he were still trying to find it. A part of me relaxed; they were merely boys on the cusp of manhood! Then that part of me stiffened up once more, realizing that there were three of them. Growing up on the farm had given me the advantage to become strong and agile, which gave me the advantage of surprise. They wouldn't expect me to be able to defend myself. But what of Dah'nelle? I had no idea if she could hold her own against these ragamuffins.

"Yes, we did. Do you know where the Oak and Staff is? We were told by Rhyben that we could go there if we needed a bed and food."

"Told you that, did he? Well, Rhyben knows a good many of us...But we all grew up here. Why would he send strangers to us?"

"Maybe because he knows that they can help us." I whirled around, which was probably the wrong thing to do, turning my back to three possible attackers to face a new one, but I figured that Dah'nelle would give me some warning if those boys attacked.

The new voice belonged to another male, this one just a shade older, with an air of authority that the others could never possess. His hair hung in his eyes, and he tossed his head back to shake it away. He'd been standing on a balcony, within easy distance to jump down, which he did. The advantage would have been his had Dah'nelle and I were winning the fight that never happened. His stride was long and sure, as if he knew every brick in the street personally. My wariness grew as he came closer; it must have shown on my face for he gave me a lop-sided grin and stopped a few feet away. "New to town, aren't ye?"

"You could say that," I replied, allowing my body to relax, but not my hands. A moment or two passed as we took assessment of one another before I allowed my fingers to extend. He seemed to come to a conclusion and relaxed as well, glancing to the boys behind me and making a small movement with his head. I turned to face them, but they were gone without a sound or trace. Perplexed, I turned around again, and he was studying Dah'nelle intently. "You're an initiate of Fortunae Cosmina?"

"Yes, I am."

"Then you'll find food and shelter at the temple. I can have someone show you the way there. You, however," he said, shifting his gaze to me, "will come with me. We have much to discuss."

"I think you are right, but first we disucss the fact that she comes with me." Dah'nelle looked startled. "You just insulted her, and you're gonna make up for it."

"How did I do that?"

"You dismissed her out of hand. You don't know what she's capable of, and you just pushed her aside. Well, she's my friend, and I won't let you treat her like that." Dah'nelle gave a soft gasp as he raised a brow.

"Well, I do apologize. She is more than welcome to stay at the Oak and Staff, but don't be fooled, she will have to work as hard as you if she wants to stay."

"I'm not afraid of work," said Dah'nelle, a strange light in her eyes. As he lead the way out of the alley, she leaned in to me and whispered, "I've never had a friend, before. Thank you."

"Truly?" I whispered back. "Well, then, today is your lucky day...!" She bit her lower lip, her eyes shimmering, and I turned away, something had brought her low like this. We followed our host in silence, each in our own thoughts as we walked thru the city streets. Finally, we reached a broad, bright building, a raucous noise emanating from within, punctuated by sudden bursts of clarity as the door was popped open, either disgorging previous customers or welcoming new members to the fracas. We went down the side alley to the back, and he held open a door that allowed heat and light out, as well as the scent of roasting meats and the sound of plates being plunked down onto a table. He inclined his head towards the opening, and I sucked in a breath and stepped over the threshold.

It was a kitchen nearly as wide as the building itself. It was attached to the back by a swinging door, as if it were an addition that someone had forgotten to put into the original floor plans. There was a wall that extended from the back of the building to support a great oven and fire pit over which rested a large pig. I could see loaves of bread baking in the open ovens, and a pot boiling with stew hanging from the spit. My mouth watered at the aromatic air, and my stomach gave me a sharp reminder that the not-quite-ripe apples we had continued to gather were sitting uneasily in my gullet. A large man was tending to the spit, turning the pig's carcass slowly, slicing pieces from its flank and side. Under the pig was a metal basket, filled with various vegetables, soaking it the melting fat from the meat. He turned as the door was shut firmly, and I winced, thinking that I looked a frightful mess. Since I had no pack, I had no spare clothes, and Dah'nelle could only do so much with her comb and my hair. "I've brought a couple of girls to help with some of the chores, Da."

"Well, will you lookie here! C'mon in, get warmed up by the fire. Nothin gonna harm you here, I won't have it." We moved closer to the spit, and his eyes sized the two of us up. "Well, now, you're in initiates' robes, aren't ye? To whom do you feel the callin' to?"

"Fortunae Cosmina," said Dah'nelle. "It's a pleasure to meet you, sir."

"Ah, dun call me "Sir," I'm no nobleman. Just call me Da, everyone does." He turned to me with a smile. "And you?"

"I'm Maya, S...Da." I'd never in my life called anyone else Da except, well, *my* Da, so it was rather awkward.

"Maya. Such a pretty name. Now, let's get something' in yer bellies before I get you started working. My son, Braedion, he knows good workers when he finds them. So we help you if you help us. Deal?" We both nodded wordlessly as we were given seats at the table and plates of food. The warm bread melted butter quickly and the hot stew was amazing. I'd had two bowlfuls before I realized that it was meant for other guests as well. I studied our new surroundings, stopping when I saw Braedion watching me. I stole glances at him while we ate, not sure what he could possibly want from us other than another pair of hands to do work around the inn that he should be doing. To my surprise, I watched as he rolled up his sleeves and began to turn the spit when his father wasn't, and taking bread out of the ovens as well as putting the raw loaves in. A young lad was hauling in dishes and placing them into a tub of soapy water, then bustling out again with another platter of food for the guests. Soaking up the last of the gravy with my bread, I popped the morsel into my mouth, rolled up my sleeves, and took my dishes to the wash tub, where I started to wash the piles of plates and bowls. Washing dishes had been a chore at home, one I didn't mind so much, and the work went quickly, for it seemed that as soon as I cleared the tub, it filled again. Dah'nelle was helping the boy, Rickard, take food out to tables and bussed back the dirty dishes. Before long, we were both red-faced and sweating, and she had to loosen the wrap about her head. Braedion watched me as I moved quickly, setting the dishes out to dry for a moment before they were swiped to be filled and taken out again. It was all beginning to blur a bit, till one of the earthen mugs slipped from my hand and bounced against the side of the tub. I snatched it out of the air before it hit the floor, and as I straightened, I nearly hit heads with Braedion, who had been reaching out to catch it, as well. We laughed a bit at the silliness of it, and I resumed washing dishes again. "Tell me about yourself, Maya."

I blinked in surprise; we'd been working in companionable silence for a while, him cooking while I washed dishes and cleaned the table and swept the floor. My mouth opened, shut, then opened again, finally snapping shut as I turned back to the wash tub. "Not much to tell, really."

"Were you running away?"

An innocent enough question, but I balked at answering it. "It wasn't the life I was meant to have."

"I see..." Another round of dishes coming in and food going out paused our conversation, then Da entered the kitchen. "Okay, I've locked the doors for the night, the last of the guests are eating, and the last of the dishes will be coming back here." Da looked around, seeing that I had been keeping up with the washing, piling the dishes neatly on the shelves. "Well, will you looky there? Looks like we found a keeper, Braedion!"

"Sure does, Da."

Da's brow furrowed. "Reminds me of someone, ya know? I'm sure that it'll come to me....." Braedion hurried forward with a steaming mug, handing it to Da.

"Here, Da, drink this. You know the healer said you needed to take a cup of tea in the morning and one at night before bed. May as well do it now, so you don't forget."

"Ah, Braedion, thank you. I trust that you and the others will clean up and lock up for the night? Don't forget to show Maya and Dah'nelle to their room. We get up pretty early around here, so be sure to rest up!" Da trundled off with his mug, taking sips of the warm liquid. I finished up the dishes, swept the floor, and tossed down a bucket of water to scrub it down. Housework was nothing new, and caring for an inn is pretty much like caring for a house. Dah'nelle joined me in scrubbing the wood, and we made quick work of it. Even Rickard helped by wiping up with towels, which we rinsed and hung out to dry near the oven. Braedion banked the fire, and shoo'ed Rickard off to bed, then lead us upstairs to our room. We passed a room where snores could be heard, and Braedion closed the door. Once in our room, I saw the clean room with its neat beds, and could hardly wait to peel off my clothing and fall onto the mattress. Then I realized that Braedion was in the room and shutting the door behind him, locking it so we wouldn't be disturbed. Dah'nelle and I exchanged startled looks, and I readied myself for a fight.

Braedion sat upon the only stool in the room beside a small table with a mirror above it. Mirrors were expensive, or so *my* Da said, which is why my mother prized the small hand-held one she I as a wedding gift from my father. I looked about, figuring that Braedion's father had to be one of the more profitable inn keepers around to have such things about. But I was more worried about the intense look Braedion was giving me. "You're quick with your hands."

The statement took me off guard. "Beg your pardon?"

"The mug that would have shattered on the floor. You were quick to catch it." My tired body was overriding my tired mind, and I sat on the edge of the bed to face him. "I need someone with quick reactions for something."

"If you're thinking of a tumble, you're going to have to look elsewhere," I growled. A look of shock came over his face, then it hardened.

"No, I don't want you in that manner!" He stood, then paced, fingers pushing thru his hair. "It's...I don't know where to begin..."

"The beginning, of course," said Dah'nelle. Braedion smiled at the advice, and nodded.

"About a month ago, this I opened not too far from here. It became all the rage, of course, because it catered to the appetites of many. Or so they said. All manner of people went to the I, and it became quite popular. Of course, there are a LOT of inns and restaraunts and the like here in Ironhill, but no one seemed to notice."

"Notice what?" I asked around a yawn.

"That people were disappearing. At first, it was the vagrants, homeless, people who would hardly be missed. But then, others began to disappear, too. One was Rickard's mother, so we took him in. Another was my sister..."

"Sister?" My sleep-longing mind tugged at something, then unraveled it. "Is that what Da meant when he said that I reminded him of someone?"

"Yes, he was beside himself with worry when she disappeared. In order to keep him together enough to run the inn, I had to ask for a special tea that was designed to deal with his memory. Specifically, to make him not remember my sister, Ambea." Braedion stopped his pacing and sat down again. "She was his world. And mine, as well. She helped out with running everything. It's been a bit of a struggle with her gone."

***

"How long ago did she disappear?" asked Dah'nelle. She seemed excited at the tale, and I fought to stifle down another yawn. I silently cursed my body and its betrayal. Life on the farm was from sun up to sundown, and it was very much sundown for me.

"It's been a week or more. We talked to the authorities, but it seems that they're in the owners' pocket. None of the people who had gone missing have been seen ever again. But I know Ambea is alive. I feel it!" He thumped his chest for emphasis, and I winced at the hard sound, thinking he was going to be bruised in the morning.

"Well, there really isn't much we can do right now. It's late and no one is open at this hour, except those places of ill-repute," I managed, rubbing my face. "We can go and look at this place before we open, here. But right now, I am too tired to even think straight!"

Braedion looked ready to argue, but my face must have shown that his death would hardly be a chore for me if I did not get sleep soon. He nodded and stood. "You are right, it would be fool-hardy to go in unprepared. I will bid you good night, and I will see if I can find something of Ambea's that might fit you, two. You seem to be about her height and weight, if not her age." He unlocked the door and paused after opening it. "I hope that you can help me find her, again." The door shut firmly behind him and I moaned and flopped over on my side.

Dah'nelle jumped to her feet. "Come on! We have to hurry!"

"What!?" I snarled from the pillow that was wrapping my head in softness. "I think we have some time..."

"But what if something was happening to her?! What if she were being held captive, or, what if she were being fed a piece at a time to the guests?"

I made a face at the thought. "A piece at a time? How?"

"You can cut off a limb, you know, and still live." The thought made my stomach roll. "When I've become an apprentice in the House of Fortune, I could learn how to heal. Healers know how to remove fingers, toes, arms and legs and still keep you alive."

THAT made me sit upright. "All right, but how will we find it? Braedion never said the name of the restaurant, it's the middle of the night, and in a city the size of Ironhill?"

"With a little bit of luck!" she said, pulling a small box from her pack. From the box, she pulled a piece of parchment with a circle inscribed upon it and a chain with a crystal at the end. I stifled a yawn as she smoothed out the parchment on the bed, holding the chain with both hands, and murmuring a prayer. I stretched and rubbed my face, then watched as the crystal began to swing on the chain, circling and circling, then it began to swing in a single direction. Soon, it was acting ilke a dog on a short rope scenting a rabbit. My brows rose as I watched, fascinated. "Think you can teach me that trick?"

"It's not a trick," whispered Dah'nelle, standing quickly and holding onto the end of the crystal's chain like a leash. "It's a prayer to Cosmina asking for assistance in finding my way. Usually, it's meant as a prayer; asking for guidance in difficult life decisions. I just modified it a bit to work for physical direction."

"Is that safe? To tamper with spells like that?"

"It is if it doesn't hurt anyone, isn't it?" The discussion was dropped as she opened the door and peered into the hall. "Let's go before anyone can stop us!" Quietly we slipped out of our room and down the hall past the occupied rooms. We went through the back, making our way out of the kitchen and into the alley, following the tugging on the crystal. We walked through the shadowed streets, and I felt the eyes of the night following our every move. I shook off the feeling, knowing that there were others who embraced the darkness. After a few turns, the crystal's chain stiffened, then went limp, swinging solemnly from Dah'nelle's fingers. "It looks like we're here."

"Here where?" I asked, looking around. There wasn't a building that seemed much like a restaurant, no matter how hard I looked. The darkness made my eyes ache for sleep and I rubbed them once again. "Are we sure we can find our way back?"

"We'll be fine. But we need to get into the restaurant." Dah'nelle slipped the crystal into her pocket. "You cirlce around to the right, I'll go left."

"Can't we wait till morning? I can barely see my hand in front of my face."

"No, I don't think we'll have much luck in the morning. Let's go!" She tugged me from the side of the building and we crossed the street to what finally looked like a restaurant. Keeping my muttering to a bare whisper, I went about to the back of the building, keeping a hand on the wall to guide me. I tripped over several bags of garbage, trying not to curse and biting my tongue in the process. If I made it around to the back without finding anything, I was going to give Dah'nelle a piece of my mind and not speak to her for days.

Chapter 3

Moonlight brushed the ground before me as clouds scudded by, and a glint of light on metal caught my eye. It was a locket on the ground, and I bent over to pick it up. The chain was caught under a bag, and I pulled. It was stuck fast, and I growled as I yanked on it again. The bags moved, one ripping around the chain, and I dropped the jewelry as I gasped for air, my tired brain and weary eyes trying to put the nightmarish scene before me into something I could grasp. Lifeless eyes bore into my face, not seeing me, or anything else, for that matter. Air burned my lungs as I tried to find a voice to scream with. I fell over backwards, the pain in my rear and hands helping to focus my fear. Yes, she was dead, but she couldn't hurt me. Not unless she was like in the stories my Da would tell me, the ones where those who had died came back to life. The longer I sat there, the less the fear gripped me, and after a few more deep breaths, I managed to crawl over to the corpse and examine her.

The body hadn't begun to smell, yet, and the other bags, obviously of other trash, masked the scent. Had the bag not ripped, no one would have been able to tell that a body had been hidden in it. The bags would have been collected and the refuse used for fertilizer. By the time the trash was opened and the body discovered, she would have been rotted beyond recognition. Save for the locket and clothing, she would have had no other way of being identified. Swallowing down my bile, I reached over again and pulled the locket away from her neck. Opening it, I saw a familiar face etched onto a piece of parchment tucked into it. My heart felt a pang of regret, and I folded the chain and tucked the jewelry into a pocket.

I stood on shaky legs, then glanced around. The feeling that I was being watched seemed to double, even triple, but I continued around to the back. There was a door similar to how Braedion's Da's inn was set up, but before I could try the latch, a hand fell upon my shoulder. Whirling around, I saw Dah'nelle put her hands up defensively as I had raised my fist to throw the first punch. We both breathed in sighs of relief, and she whispered, "We need to get into the building to look around."

"Well, I was about to open the door when you startled me," I hissed back. Turning back to the door, I tried the knob and was slightly surprised to find it unlocked. We exchanged a worried look, and swung the door open. Creeping in, we looked about the kitchen, finding it quite spotless, as if they never used it. I frowned as we explored by the light of the embers in the fireplace. It was puzzling, for there was a fire, and several kettles on hooks, and as I tilted one, liquid poured out, smelling aromatically like tea. Puzzled, I pulled a mug from the shelf, and poured some into it. Without honey to sweeten it, the tea was awful, and I spit it out. Putting the tea aside, I made my way to the door of the inn, following Dah'nelle. "There's tea in the kettles near the fire, but nothing else being prepared. Perhaps this is simply a tea house?"

"I don't think so. I saw some herbs being stored, and most of them I recognize as herbs used for meditation and memory."

"Memory...." I frowned as I thought back to our conversation with Braedion, and I reminded Dah'nelle about it. "Didn't he say that he was using a special tea for his father to forget his sister had disappeared?"

"Yes. Sometimes, it's better to forget, even for a little while."

"What if he's not doing it for a little while?"

"What? Are you suggesting that he's perhaps drugging his father to forget that he had a sister? To what purpose?"

"I don't know. What would he have to gain from it?"

"Well, you can brew a tea to forget a person or an event; it's tricky, and it takes an expert with herbs to do it, but you can do it."

"Could the memory loss become permanent?"

"I don't know..." Her voice trailed off, and I saw that she was staring behind me. I whipped around to see Braedion standing behind me. "Cosmina...!"

"What are you two doing here!?" Braedion demanded in a hoarse whisper. "I thought you two were sleeping! Instead I hear you two sneaking out and coming here!"

"Why are you really drugging your father? Are you really trying to protect him or are you trying to make him forget that he has a daughter? Or is she really your sister?" I accused, snarling as I stepped between him and Dah'nelle. I felt that I could tangle him somehow in a brawl so that Dah'nelle could get away and hopefully make it to the temple of Cosmina.

"Yes she's my sister and I was going to come here and see if I could scout the area for you to come in disguise and find her. But here I find you two skulking about!"

"How do we know that you aren't drugging your father to forget about your sister? I found that body outside, how do we know that you aren't planning the same for your father?" His moonlit skin paled even more at the mention of the body, and I pressed on. "Is that too detailed for you? Didn't think that your sister will end up in a bag as so much trash?" I pushed on his chest, and he gave a step. "This is pretty sick, even for you...!" Dah'nelle took a step forward to grab my hands...

...and fell limply to the floor. Braedion stiffened, then he, too, crumpled to the floorboards. A figure stood there, no eyes, a slotted nose and a mouth opened wide in a silent scream, calmly holding out a hand towards me. There was a flash of confused horror, then the darkness mercifully claimed me and I slept.

***

My body was heavy. Too heavy. I couldn't lift my arms, much less breathe. Foggily, my brain reacted to the lack of air, sending my body into a panicked state, causing me to flail against the weight that pinned me down. Apparently I hit a soft spot, because I heard a grunt and dark mutterings. Another feeble hit, this time with a little leg thrown about, and the weight rolled off of me, cursing a bit louder. I took a gulp of air, thankful that my body was able to move. Save for my leg, which seemed to be pinned by another body. Pulling free from the pile, I noted that we were not alone in a stark room with one window set high into the wall. I looked about groggily, spotting Dah'nelle sleeping near my feet. Braedion was kneeling next to a girl, touching her hair and whispering to her. I could only assume it was his sister who looked at him slightly perplexed, as if she were trying to place his features. Taking in more of my surroundings, I looked at the gaunt faces and thin bodies of the other people in the room. Several were weeping openly, as if nothing but sadness consumed them, and others were staring off blindlessly, drool seeping from one or both corners of their mouths. Another type of horror gripped me as I fought to remember why we were in this room. I reached over and shook Dah'nelle awake, letting her stretch and yawn as I stood to study our surroundings.

Braedion turned towards me, his eyes grave and angry. "It is as I feared. We have to leave this place before what's happened to them happens to us."

"What's happened to them?" I whispered, as if afraid to disturb the confused peace here.

"They can't remember. I've asked some of the ones who seemed sane enough to answer how they got here. What they can remember is very little of how they got here, but they can't seem to remember anything else."

"And how did most of them get here?"

"A few of them remember that they were looking for something or someone, but beyond that..." he shrugged.

Dah'nelle was examining one of the drooling prisoners, waving a hand in their face and even lifting their arm, only to watch as the arm stayed extended into the air. "I've seen this type of sickness only a few times before. The patient doesn't react to anyone, or anything. The body functions, but the mind is gone...blank."

"So there is no one in there to tell the body when to eat, or when to shyte," said Braedion, confirming with Dah'nelle. Her nod caused his face to darken even more. "What of the weeping ones?"

"Give me a moment to find out." Dah'nelle approached a weeping woman who reminded me of my mother. I felt a pang of guilt as I thought of her, and how she would have reacted to my leaving the house without so much as a note. I was going to leave one, explaining that I wanted to have something more than just the life of a farmer's brood mare, but I don't think she would have understood me. Or, even worse, she would have understood, but could not do anything to change that fate for me.

Dah'nelle came back to us, her face set and anger in her eyes. "She can't stop crying because all she can do is remember the things she'd done in her past that were saddening. She cannot remember a single happy occurance in her life."

"No happiness?" It sounded incredulous, even to my ears. I ran my hands thru my hair, tugging at the strands to jog my memories. "What's going on here? A tea house of lost memories?"

"No," said Braedion. "A tea house of stolen memories." The confusion was probably plain on my face, for he continued. "There are creatures in the world that feed off of things other than food. Some feed on human flesh; others, human blood." He turned to look into the face of his sister, Ambea. "I think these creatures feed off of memories. First, they take the happy ones, the ones filled with family, friends, loved ones. Then those moments of peace, where you are content with life. Then the sad ones, then any memories left over...." Looking to the prisoner with the arm in the air, he finished with, "..till there's nothing left, except so much blood and flesh."

Anger filled me, and I turned to slap my hand against the wall. The sting in my palm helped me to focus the anger, and I pressed my head to the wall. "Before we were taken, I saw one of them. I coudln't tell if it was man nor woman, but it had no eyes, barely a nose, and a hole for a mouth. That was all I remember, then everything went black." I turned to Dah'nelle and Braedion, and neither of them registered recognition to my description. "How do they feed? And how long have they been here? How many people fell victim to their needs, and how are they luring the victims into the tea house?"

"They have to have allies. I know I certainly wouldn't want to have tea here if the servers had no faces!" claimed Dah'nelle. She was toying with something at her neck, and in the dim light, I saw flashes on metal. I watched, fascinated for a moment, then shook my head. "We need to get out of here and alert the authorities."

"I tried the authorities, they didn't believe me," said Braedion. "We'll have to give them proof."

"There's a body in the alleyway, that's at least worth an investigation. If they were to explore the tea house, I'm sure they'd find this room and all those here."

"So how do we get out of here?" The light glanced off the pendant Dah'nelle wore, catching my eye and making me stare at the small trinket. I shook my head again; I had to be more tired than I thought for something as small as bits of light to...

My arrested look alerted Braedion. "You've thought of something?"

"Yes....how do they see if they have no eyes?" They both wore perplexed looks for a moment before I pressed on. "If they don't have any eyes to see with, how do they see? They have to sense you, but how? If they are draining memories from someone, then they see without eyes...."

"I think I understand," said Dah'nelle, getting excited. "These creatures use thoughts to see their victims and others around them. If you're thinking of a happy moment in time, a memory, that's their food and that's how they hunt. They sense your thoughts and they seek you out."

"That has to be it. So in order to escape, we need to not think about anything. Not remember."

"That's impossible," scoffed Braedion. "You can't NOT feel anything, much less NOT think. Unless you were asleep, and even then, you could dream, and that has as much emotion as being awake and remembering things that made you happy or sad."

"Asleep while awake. That's brilliant!" I gave Dah'nelle an odd look, wondering if the creatures that held us captive had been able to worm their way into her mind already. "It's like meditating; you reach another state of consciousness, one where your emotions and memories are held in check, and clarity of thought comes thru!"

"That seems to be the only way out, then," said Braedion. "Can you do it? You're an acolyte of Cosmina....surely you know of some meditations that will allow you to do what you've said?"

"I've never been good at meditation. I could do it for only a few minutes, then I come out of it. It takes years of practice to get that good."

"But there are ways around that...you can put people into a trance; I've seen it done at the travelling faire."

"How did they do it?" asked Braedion.

"I--I'm not sure," I admitted, giving a small shrug. "I remember that the man told the woman that she was asleep, and that when she opened her eyes she would be asleep, but be able to move. He made her move about, answer questions, but when he "awakened" her, she couldn't remember anything that she had done."

"Do you think you can recreate it?"

"Well, I know that he told her to relax, cloes her eyes, keep breathing, and that she should open her eyes and do as he told her, then the made her go back to sleep, then woke her from the trance."

"I think I can do that to you," said Dah'nelle. "I think that I can put you under just enough to take some of my simpler commands, then you will wake up."

"It's worth a shot. How should we do this?"

The next few minutes, we talked about what we wanted to accomplish; about how I was to come and rescue them since--in theory!--I would be rendered invisible to our captors. I nodded and laid down onto the stone floor. My body was both tired and ready to move at the same time. I listened to Dah'nelle's voice, how calmly she told me to let myself drift and sleep, that before long, I would be back at the inn and enjoying some wonderful food, but that first, I must complete my tasks....

Chapter 4

Bodies shuffled past me, and I watched thru dispassionate eyes as Dah'nelle and Braedion were herded thru the door and away from the room. I looked at the door they left by, listening to the protests of those who were not quite wiped by these creatures.

I knew I should be angry...I knew I should lash out and probably kill all of them to end this nightmare, however I was not interested in these things as I rose to the door and tried the latch. A door that was supposed to be locked and prevent the others from escaping was allowing me to do so. I stored the information away in some part of my mind; it could be analyzed later. For now, it seemed to be alright for me to leave the holding cell and make my way down the hall to the main parlor room. I saw several patrons sitting around the tables, all sipping tea. Again, I could not feel anger at these people who were sipping quietly from their cups, enjoying the tiny pastries set about on huge plates. A few glanced at me, startled, and whispered behind their hands. But I was not seeing them, at least, not fully. I was busily watching the faceless beings wandering unchecked about the room. None of the patrons enjoying their tea seemed to notice as they wandered from table to table, pausing behind tea drinkers every so often. I watched as one of the creatures came close to a woman, and a wisp of what looked like steam entered its mouth. Another creature joined the first, and they seemed to confer with one another in regards to the person they had sampled from.

I turned away, and headed for the kitchen. There, several people were bustling about, readying tea services on trays and baking the delicate pastries that would be consumed with the tea. One of the cooks was bent over a large pot, pouring herbs into the water and stirring, tasting, then adding something else. Aromatic scents filled the air near the pot, but again, this was not what I was looking for. A few of the servers glanced at me, but it seemed that no one wanted to stop me as of yet.

There was a door off to the side that Dah'nelle and myself had missed last night in the dark. We also had no clue what we were looking for at that time, so it was dismissed out of hand, but now I strode towards the door with purpose, and lifted the latch to enter.

The room was dark, lit only by a few candles set in glasses. There was weeping and the air stank of sour sweat and fear. I looked left and right, at the people who were shackled to the wall. Wide-eyed terror showed on some of the faces, and a blank stare were on others, and some were even smiling, remembering some of the happier moments in their lives. Dah'nelle and Braedion were there, eyes wide open, staring off into the soft darkness, recalling details of their lives for the nourishment of these creatures. One approached Dah'nelle, the sucking vacuum of its mouth mere inches away from her face. Dah'nelle's breathing quickened, her mouth working as if to summon a scream, but no sound was coming out.

Some part of my mind registered what was happening to her, and there seemed to be a scrabbling sensation at the back of my head, as if my conscious mind wanted to come to the fore and get me screaming. Instead, I walked calmly up to Dah'nelle, cupping her cheek and turning her head to me. She stared past me as if I weren't there, and some part of me knew that she *couldn't* see me, due to some unseen force blocking her mind. I pulled my hand back, and let it fly across her cheek, the sound of my hand striking her ringing out over the cries of the tortured.

Everything seemed to still in that moment, and Dah'nelle shook her head clear of the fog in her mind as I turned to the creature, swinging at it, and feeling my hand pass thru what felt like the mud from the road, something soft, passable, though sticky in a way. The creature made no sound, but retreated, backing away from Dah'nelle. I turned and worked at the pins that held the cuff around her wrist, loosening them to allow her to pull herself free as I turned again to face the creature. It cast about, as if trying to find me, lashing at the air feebly and connecting with some of the other prisoners. Everytime it hit a prisoner, that person would scream out in terror, their fear triggered by the creature's confusion. Where it touched a person, a bruise would appear, and the same detached part of my mind noted that and kept out of range, though I would dart in and strike at a part of the creature, keeping it distracted from Dah'nelle and Braedion, whom she had managed to free and awaken as I moved about the room, dodging the beast.

A few moments later, a voice sounded out behind me, "Oi! What're you doin' here!?" Turning, I saw one of the servers had come into the room to investigate the cries of the prisoners. Distracted, I didn't avoid the next blow, and the wall that kept my emotions in check shattered under that touch, and I crumpled to the floor, screaming...

...it was dark, so dark I couldn't see, but I could hear it...them...scratching, scratching, always scratching...nibbling away at the sacks of grain...nibbling away at the bread...leaving behind feces and piss...beady little eyes staring at me, some black as night and some red as burning coals...they get bolder, coming closer. I can hear them...can't see them...I can feel them...smell them...their fur brushing against my hands, my legs...feel them, sharp claws and sharper teeth, biting, nibbling, taking their time as their teeth rended my skin to ribbons, nuzzling into my warm, wet, bleeding flesh. Bleeding from the bites, the scratches, bleeding out onto the floor....

...kicking out, my foot strikes something, and the connection is lost. I flail in the grip of someone, pushing back with my head and hearing an oath as something warm flows into my hair. My hands grab something, anything, and I pull it to my mouth, biting hard and hearing more shouts. Other voices, questions being asked, the prisoners screaming incoherently, confusion, someone grabbing me, dragging me as I stumbled across the floor, fear spurring me onwards, skin twitching from the imagined bites, had to get away, find the light, there, thru the door, blinded by the sudden glare of day, stumbling further till I couldn't stand any longer, and I hit the ground...

***

Surrounded by an unfamiliar softness, I nestled down into the blankets a little further, my hand brushing against my face as I turned over. I smiled into the pillow; I had never felt anything so soft and comfortable. Then I frowned, cracking my eyes open. The pillows on my bed at home were nothing more than a folded winter blanket, but this was....luxurious. As my eyes focused, I looked about, noting the other bed in the room, the small vanity, and the occupied chair pulled close to my bed. There was a book laying on the corner of the bed I laid in, and the dark hair of Braedion as it laid on his folded arms. His breathing told me that he was asleep, and I tried to quietly shift away so that I could turn onto my side to watch him. My movements moved the bed, and woke him anyways, as he sat up suddenly, looking at me with the same confusion I had before, then smiled. "Well, I was wondering when you would awaken...!"

I returned his smile as I nestled in again. "I didn't know I was sleeping."

"It was hard to tell. When we pulled you out of the tea house and brought you back here, you were incoherent; babbling about bites and alternating between screaming and crying. We couldn't do anything for you but then you suddenly collapsed into a deep sleep. The physician took a look at you and said that we were to let your mind and body heal themselves. That whatever you were suffering from would work itself out."

"Did you believe him?"

Braedion snorted. "Not a chance. Dah'nelle asked Cosmina for a favor and found someone who had dealt with this before. Apparently, you weren't the only one to have fought these things and lived to tell the tale."

I shuddered at the thought, and had to ask, "What were those things?"

"Meme-o-rai," he said. "They feed off the memories and emotions of humans. They don't exist on this plane, or, at least, only long enough to feed off of humans and other creatures. Somehow, someone must have struck a bargain with these creatures to keep them handy."

"Why?" I asked, working my way into a sitting position. My body felt sore, reminding me of the time I had a fever that lasted for days, and I was unable to eat or drink very much, and moving had hurt so badly, all I could do was lay there. My mother had prayed hard to keep me alive. Another pang of guilt, and a plan formed in my mind to let her know that I was alive.

"In a city this big, there are a lot of secrets to keep. The Meme-o-rai can erase memories, draining them from a human like a mosquito drains blood. Of course, sometimes, the Meme-o-rai erases the wrong memories...or just doesn't stop draining them. Before long, the person no longer recalls who they are, where they come from..."

"Ye gods, your sister...! Is she alright?"

"Yes, we saved her before she forgot everything in her life." Braedion gathered my hands into his. "For saving her, I owe you everything."

"Does your father remember her?"

"Yes, yes he does! I didn't dose him with his tea in the morning, and when he saw her..." He bowed his head to compose himself, then continued. "Thank you, Maya. They seem like small words, but thank you."

I mustered a smile, giving his hands a squeeze to command his attention, and murmured, "You can pay me back by leaving the room...I need to use the chamber pot..."

Chapter 5

Later that evening, with Braedion's help, I managed to wobble down the stairs to the main common room. There was a cheer as cups were raised to my bravery, and Dah'nelle grabbed me tightly into a hug. Ambea shyly smiled at me, serving me my first real meal in a while. Rickard came to me, and I handed him the locket from his mother's neck. He smiled, hugging me tightly, whispering his thanks. Da had taken him in when he saw him wandering the streets on his own, giving him a sense of purpose and a place to stay. He thrived in this makeshift family, and I was glad for it. Braedion leaned in and conspired with me to help me get proper training to fight so that the next time something like this happened, I wouldn't be so useless. I sputtered indignantly around a mouthful of stew, wiping my chin as I fixed him with a glare that only made him laugh.

The door to the inn banged open, silencing the room. A tall man stood in the frame, skin dark as polished wood, his clothing loose and dusty, the color of fall leaves. He practically shimmered in the light of the inn as he walked to the wall that was covered in papers. I hadn't noticed the message board before now, and he used one of the nails to hang a piece of parchment onto the wood. He walked out in the same stony silence he had come in with, and the rest of the patrons started up their mutterngs once more.

I stood up and went to the message board, pulling the new notice from the wall. There was a portrait on the page, with the words: WANTED, DEAD OR ALIVE. The face was menacing, to say the least: dark eyes, a wide jaw, hair that looked like it was pulled back tightly. I brought the paper to the table, laying it out and studying it as I ate the food brought to me by Dah'nelle. "What are you doing with that?" she asked.

"Well, if we're to earn our keep, what with Ambea being back, now, we may as well make ourselves useful!"

"By going after a wanted criminal?" queried Braedion.

"Well, yes."

"Do you even know where to find him?"

"Sure. With a little help from Cosmina." I winked at Dah'nelle and she shook her head, gathering empty dishes and cups and taking them back to the kitchen.

"Do you *really* think you can do it?" Braedion asked, eying me. "You barely got out of the last mess of trouble."

I snorted and waved a hand at him, already forming a plan. "Details, details!"

The End

About the Author

Mary is an up and coming author and mother who decided to join our project in order to help expand the Chronicles of Ollundra setting. Mary lives with her one child in Louisiana in the USA.

Withertale

By

Péter Holló-Vaskó

Prologue

"Men are felled by what they fall to believe in."

- Eluveitie: Origins, track: Ogmios

The Sleeper was first. He knew no beginning, as he knows no end.

He dreamed of creation, he dreamed of our world. Ant thus our world was born.

But even before that, the Sleeper was tortured by nightmares, dark visions of all the suffering, fear, hate and chaos in the world he intended to create.

His nightmares woke. That is how the firstborn, the Old Gods were born.

The world came into existence then with all the beauty and people the Sleeper dreamed into it.

And the nightmares of the creator, the Old Gods descended upon us in fire, despair, pain and death.

Yet the people of Ollundra shouted their desperate wishes upon the sky. They dreamed of peace, understanding, joy and life. They wished for nothing but healing for their burning world.

Their yearning entered the Sleeper's mind and his dreams of compassion gave birth to the Gods of Order. These young gods saw Ollundra and all its people suffer under the rage of the Old Ones. Righteous anger burned in their hearts as they fell into ranks under the leadership of Dariasul, the God of Innocence and Shi'Ara, Goddess of Creation and Healing.

These two led the other gods into aCelestial War that ravaged the very fabric of existence. But in the end the Old Gods were utterly crushed; and they were gods no more, just mere Howling in the Winds of the Dream.

The Gods of Order rule ever since and continue to watch over us all. You do not need to fear your nightmares, my child, you need not dread the Howling, for it is no more than an echo of a legion of mad spirits murdered for their ruthless evil. Ollundra is healed and will stay this way for all eternity. May the Sleeper dream well.

The Catechism of the Wind, written by Dreamcaster Fa'aethon, First Primarch of the Catechumenate

Chapter 1: Promises

Maazer was only fifteen the day he lost everything.

Of course, he didn't have much to lose. Nobody living in the Ruffian District of Corona had much to begin with, and Maazer tended to count himself among the poorest of the poor. Yet when he woke in the mornings and looked at the girl sleeping soundly next to him, he sometimes felt richer than the Primarch of the Catechumenate.

The girl was a year younger than him, and as he frequently told her, she would be a real beauty, had she been born under a nobleman's roof and not on the streets of the Ruffian District. The girl would smile and tell him that there is no roof more beautiful than the Sleeper's sky, and that she is perfectly content with their life.

Yet Maazer knew he was right. Constant hunger and life on the streets takes a toll on the health and body of even the strongest. She was not ugly or particularly ill – but when he looked at her, he didn't just see how she was – but what she *could* be. And he was worried for her.

He felt responsible for her. Having a sister does that to a boy, even if that boy hates responsibility and despises everyone who acts responsibly.

On one night he got themselves a loaf of bread and a big slice of cheese. They were sitting on the Bridge of Hopes and enjoyed the tickling of the water of river Eyron on their feet.

"Hey, Rini" the boy began.

"Hmm?" his sister regarded him surprised. It wasn't like him to just trail off in the middle of a sentence. "What's up, Maaz?"

The boy sighed. The bright blue eyes of the girl, her long brown hair… she reminded him of their mother.

A mother they lost a long while ago. Life on the streets destroyed her, just as it was slowly killing Rini too. He had to act, and he knew it.

"We'll leave Corona next spring" he said.

Rini laughed. Her voice made the heavens smile, Maaz was sure of it.

"Don't be ridiculous, big brother. Where would we go?"

"Into the Monastery. I could work on the fields and you could help out in the kitchen. We'd have a roof over our heads. Think about it! Honest work, no more cold, no more hunger. No more running from the city guard…"

"You have it all planned out" she took her feet out of the river and watched as drops of water dipped back from her toes.

"Rini, I just want a better life for you. Nothing more."

"You are the best in Shadow's company. Maybe even in the whole District. You really think he's going to let you go?"

"He will. Shadow's not stupid, he's not going to seek trouble with the

Monastery. He was more than once saved by a healer of theirs. He's not going to risk it."

Rini's brows went into a frown. Her slender fingers threaded in her hair, which was a sure sign of her being afraid.

"This is dangerous talk, Maaz. I'm… I'm not sure of this."

"Come on, sis. I bet you don't want to end up like Ro'ana, being employed by Velvet and all."

Judging by the grimace she made, he was right.

"I'm not that pretty."

"Maybe. Not *yet* anyways. One or two years, a nice womanly dress from Velvet, a few months of living and eating healthily with her girls… and you would outshine the Princess, little sister."

He won, he could see it on her face, he just had to press on.

"I plan to leave after I paid back Shadow every single coin he gave us. He will not complain."

"But you know nothing of working with plants or animals. And I can't cook." the girl said and plunged her sandals into the river. The quickly rushing water almost took them out of her hands.

"Yet. Don't you worry. We can figure it out. After all, how hard can it be?"

"Aren't you too optimistic?"

"Not at all. But we're leaving this cursed city, or die trying."

Watching his sister enjoy the mild water and the food, he had no idea how right he was about that.

Chapter 2: The Smile of the Sleeper

The Market Road was the main street that led through the Ruffian District or, officially called, Nistagon Quarter. It started at the Gate of Corona and went straight to the Inner Gate leading to the Isterion Quarter, home to the Catechumenate and the wealthy of Corona.

Maazer never ever went through any of the two gates, the Ruffian District was the only place he knew.

Fitting, he thought, sitting in the dirt, wearing dirty rags, with a tin mug in his hands. *I'm quite the ruffian, so why not? Acting as a beggar, while my sister robs those who come to me driven by compassion... yes, I'm nothing more than a damn ruffian.*

Conscience however was a luxury he could not afford himself. Not yet, at least.

He caught a glimpse of Rini, stalking around like a professional thief. They would switch roles now and then, and the day he lost everything, Maaz was due to play the beggar.

Everything was as usual: the same people, doing the very same things they do every day: workers walking towards their posts, travellers looking around in awe of the grand city, a group of pilgrims clad in robes once pure white, now grey with the filth of the roads.

Maaz eyed the pilgrims hungrily. Those coming to seek the blessing of the Primarch were always a good target.

But not today. The weary group marched on towards the Inner Gate, eager to get to the Catechumenate for the daily Catechism Reading Ceremony.

After the pilgrims, the street quieted down somewhat and the heat of the summer seemed to melt the stones. Even the craftsmen and other vendors sat down in the shades, abandoning their wares on their rugs.

Maaz noticed his sister steal a small piece of cheese and some plums. *Girl's getting reckless.* Maybe the heat did it to her, or she was getting impatient. It was never a good idea to steal from somebody selling in the Ruffian District as many of them started out as thieves themselves and still remembered some of the tricks. Also, every one of them carried something called a *messer*, a blade almost as long as the outstretched hand of Rini from her shoulder to her fingernails. The parallel is fitting, it can be used to remove a limb without much difficulty.

Maaz yawned. Shadow will be so darn pissed. So far, nothing…

…then a flicker in the wind, a burst of colours, a smile on the Sleeper's face.

There were four of them. The whole world knew and feared their unnaturally shining, white cloaks and the blue symbols sewn on them.

Everyone turned their faces away, when they saw the silver rings (two or three on each finger), or the chains that connect the diadems on their foreheads with the steel collars on their necks.

The Confessors of the Catechumenate, or as they were rather called, the battlemages incited dread wherever they went. Only a fool would have looked under the white hoods of the holy warriors.

Maaz himself turned away his face, but not before noticing the girl walking carelessly between the four battlemages. She was a sight for sure: her long, red hair was reaching towards the earth in a hundred hungry braids, like the roots of a precious flower, her brown tunic and short skirt as alien as it could be.

The boy had never seen anyone with red hair like this, nor could he imagine a reason for battlemages to escort her like this. He fixed his gaze on the tin cup he was holding and hoped for the group to pass as soon as possible.

A shadow fell over him. He looked up – straight into the bluish green eyes of the girl who was now crouched before him.

Her face was like the Sleeper's sky, decorated by dozens of tiny freckles, her rich lips produced a smile Maaz liked more than anything ever before.

"Are you a person they call a 'beggar'?" she asked him. Her voice strangely deep. Maaz nodded, noting that the girl was not wearing a shoe or a sandal, yet her feet seemed completely clean. She wore rings on her toes and more than ten anklets on each leg, just like a mass of colourful bracelets on her knuckles. Her skin was as white as that of a princess.

"Do not dally" one of the mages warned her in a strict, yet cautious tone.

"I just wish to help this poor soul" the girl smiled at the Confessor. She turned back to Maaz. "Would you wish for a gift from me?"

"Certainly… my lady."

The redhead laughed heartily.

"Then one shall be given to you."

She shook her head, so her braids gave way to her hands. She reached to the back of her neck, to untie one of her many necklaces.

A small, silver medallion fell into her hand. She reached out and put it straight into the boy's palm. Her fingertips were warm, her nails painted green. Maaz has never seen something like that.

"Keep it" she whispered so silently that only he could hear, while looking him in the eyes "and wear it proudly. It helps you dream well."

As she straightened out to rejoin the battlemages, someone bumped into her. Maazer's heart almost stopped. *Rini! You fool of a girl! Not now!*

One of the battlemages let out a horrifying shout, a cry of power. A blast of heat and light hit Maaz in the face, and he saw a tiny, ragged figure fly away and clash into the dust.

All of the district seemed to be silent, as the mage lowered his glowing hand, the magical light finally dying out.

The broken body didn't move in the dust.

"We move out" one of the Confessors snapped, as he helped the girl to her feet.

She shrugged, looking at Maaz, quickly grabbing two mages by their hands to keep herself from falling.

Off they went.

Maaz waited a few heartbeats – each and every one an eternity for him. Then, as the four battlemages led off the girl, he darted to his sister.

Rini was hit hard by the magic. Blood streaked from her nose and eyes, one of her hands was broken, but she was breathing.

And in her palm she was still holding whatever she took from the redhaired girl.

Maaz dragged her into a small, dark alley to avoid unnecessary attention.

"Rini, little sister" he said, shaking her shoulders. "Rini, wake up!"

There was no response. Maaz felt a sudden rush of terror flashing through him, a terror of being alone, of losing the only thing that really mattered to him.

He drew his knife as somebody grabbed him from behind.

"It's all right, my young friend" the newcomer said "I have come here to help you."

"In my experience that usually means to 'help you for a fee', sir" the boy turned to the man. He saw a bearded man with a concerned look, who was wearing the brown and yellow cloak of the healers of Shi'Ara. On an ordinary day, Maaz would never doubt the man wearing the holy uniform.

But this was not an ordinary day. This was the day he lost everything.

"Can you help her?" he demanded. "If not, get lost already!..."

"Of course I can! I'm a healer…"

"Healer my…"

"She was struck by the Confessors, wasn't she? Just let me examine her!"

He pushed Maaz away with such passion that the boy already knew the old man spoke the truth. When the healer put his hand on Rini's forehead and muttered the sacred magical words Sh'i Ara herself taught the first of his order, Maaz didn't need confirmation anymore.

Yellow light shone through between the healer's fingers. He frowned and looked genuinely concerned.

"We must bring her to our safe house" the old man sighed wearily, removing his palm from the girl's forehead. "This… this wound requires help."

"Can you heal her there?"

"I don't know. I don't think so. I will ask my brothers to deliver her to the Monastery. The lord abbot has the necessary power and capacity to save your sister."

Maaz felt a sudden rush of blood into his face. He felt revealed, out in the open; his plan to remove her sister and himself to the monastery all of a sudden so close to being fulfilled! Did the Sleeper really smile at him today?

There was just one obstacle.

"There is a debt I need to settle, before I can go with her" the boy offered. He had no idea how he would pay Shadow back, but first things first, he had to save her sister and think about criminal overlords later.

"Her healing will take time. She won't disappear from the Monastery before you can get to her."

"Let's bring her to your safe house then."

The old man had remarkable strength left in him, he took the girl in his arms with ease.

"Follow me, young man" he said, not noticing the shiny little trinket falling from the unconscious girl's hand. Maaz caught it midair, casting a quick glimpse.

It was a bracelet, judging by its length: some sort of small token made of a blue stone on a chain that looked like gold. Seriously! Gold! Rini really has a talent for this line of work. Maaz managed to bite the piece and it was soft. He never bit gold before – but this metal felt different from everything he ever touched. Could it be?...

Now he had an idea how to pay Shadow his dues.

Chapter 3: Hunting Shadows

Rini was still unconscious when the healers in the safe house took her in. Maaz was scared at first, being deprived of her sister and only companion, but the old man assured him she will be all right with his brothers, who were already preparing her for the journey into the mountains.

"I myself have some business to attend to in the city" he told Maaz. "I figured we could stick together as long as we wrap our things up? What say you?"

"You will take me to the Monastery?" Maaz demanded.

"Yes. After we both did what we have to."

"Fine by me" Maaz stretched out a hand to the healer "They call me Maazer. My sister's Rini."

"And I am Emerich, pleased to meet you, Maazer. So, where to?"

"I have some… friends in the district. I have goodbyes to say."

"I understand. Let us meet here, in the evening, then?"

"Let it be sometime after midnight."

"Those seem to be long goodbyes you have to say."

The boy gave him a sharp look.

"Some of my friends are… what can I say. Night animals."

"Night predators, you mean?"

"That is dangerous talk."

"Yes, I reckon it might be…" the healer eyed the young thief wearily.

"Right… here, sometime after midnight."

"I'll be around" the boy slid away, hiding his face under the hood.

Getting to see Shadow was a pretty hard thing to do.

Getting Shadow do what you wanted was almost impossible.

Getting away from Shadow before you paid back everything you owe him (and with interest too!) was relatively easy compared to that. And very, utterly dangerous.

Chapter 4: Don't Lie to Him

"Ye don' jus' go an' meet Shadow, ye igno'ant li'l scum!" One-Eyed Josey was still going on about his usual homily about the sanctity of the lord of the Ruffian District. Maaz knew better than stop him.

"Yer stupidity knoweth no bounds, mate" Old Haggard added, mimicking the style of the Catechumens remarkably well. He had a reputation of doing it well, he was caught multiple times impersonating priests. His lack of fingers on his left hand spoke of those times – as did the legendary amount of money the innkeepers of the district owed him to this very day. Maaz thought Old Haggard had enough to buy a house, maybe even a manor. And not in the Ruffian District, too.

"I know, but I do have to see Shadow today" Maaz told them with a weary sigh. He tried to play his only card. "I owe him, as you both surely know well. And today I will pay him back."

"Alas, I sayeth unto Thee…" Old Haggard frowned as the words penetrated the thick mist of cheap beer that clouded his mind "Wait… what?"

"Please, sir Josey" One-Eyed was anything but a sir, but it never hurt to be polite, now, did it?

"Repay him" the bartender examined him with his only eye critically. "With what, if I, humble businessman I am, cannot even consider doing so?"

"Aye!" Haggard finally found his voice. "Ye, young little bastard, answer thine kind host."

"That's none of your business. Now, do you notify him or not?"

The bartender did not think for long. The kid's request was truly unique. Ask to see Shadow without a proper reason, and you lose a limb. Ask to see him and lie about your reason – and you might end up at the bottom of the Eyron before the next Catechism Reading Ceremony.

And they held those very often.

"Sit tight" One-Eyed grunted. "His answer will come to me. And ye know, if ye…"

"I know, if I trick him or lie to him, I'm going swimming. Hell, Josey, you speak as if I wasn't living here."

"Pa'on me fo' even tryin' to help" the bartender waved, and yelled out for his boy.

It was not easy to see Shadow. But there was no passing the city gates of Corona without his consent.

Chapter 5: I Am Autumn

The Confessor stretched out his hand to help the redhead to climb the last few steps into the Catechumenate.

"You have my thanks" the girl smiled.

"I'll rather have none of that, *ashkar*" the mage answered, as he let her hand go, as if she was inflected by the plague itself.

The girl smiled, as she strode on, the four Confessors trying to keep up with her.

Her grin broadened. They were as much her prisoners as she was theirs.

As they entered the private sanctum of the Catechumenate of Order, they found the Primarch kneeling before the Statue of All Gods in prayer. His Holiness was chanting the sacred words of the Catechism of the Fire.

And they, the Lords of Order rule over us, they watch over our cleanest feelings and desires. They purify our intents if we ask for it, just as they purified Ollundra from the filth of the Old Gods. They reduce our sinful wishes into nothingness, just as they reduced the dark ones into no more than a Howling in the Dreams of the Sleeper. Rejoice now, as your darkness comes to an end in the fires of the Sleeper's goodwill.

He rose, as the group approached him.

"Your Holiness" the four Confessors, almost omnipotent wielders of power presented a genuflection in perfect unison. The girl stood upright in their midst, looking at the Primarch with her smug smile, playing with one of her bracelets.

"Is this the child?" He wasn't afraid of her, stepped up to the girl, and raised her head by touching her chin.

"Yes, your Holiness" the leader of the mages rose to answer him. "She is the one."

"Child, are you afraid?"

"I am the daughter of the Dream. I know no fear."

"I'm sorry for you. For what you will face now…"

"… is something you call the Catechism of Fire? Come on, old man, burn me, if you dare!"

The mage captain shook as if he was hit in the face.

"The darkness is deep in this one" the Primarch whispered, narrowing his eyes. "It might even be a greater nightmare. Stay calm, my warriors, you are trained to destroy things like the one that inhabits this girl's body."

The redhead didn't stop smiling.

"Please, old man, don't exorcise me…"

"We will do exactly that, so you can no longer torment this wretched young creature" the Primarch answered. "Bring her to the altar. And you, demon of the Sleeper's dream, feel his benevolent smile, and begone, before we even begin. It will spare you a lot of pain."

"In your dreams, old man."

She was supposed to be weakening as they neared the altar of the Gods of Order. Lesser demons, the weaker nightmares that tormented the dream of the Sleeper would have already fled, but she was walking among the four mages as if she was one of them.

The Primarch was not afraid. He has faced greater nightmares before. This one… cannot be much different.

"Oh Sleeper" he began the chant of Fire. "Grant us your holy fire and…"

"Blah blah blah" the redhead rolled her eyes instead of backing down like lesser nightmares do. "Will you priests never shut up?!"

She moved with surprising agility towards the Primarch.

The four mages acted in unison, they lunged forward to ensure the safety of their high priest, their will striking at the girl.

"No."

They froze mid-air. The Primarch raised an eyebrow. A demon stopping four mages? That, by all accounts was impossible.

"The touch of this body" she was chanting "is my touch. And what you are feeling now…"

She stepped to one of the paralysed mages, eyeing him with vivid joy on her face.

"… it is called despair. Feel it! Live it! Embrace it! Your despair is so sweet…"

The fear of the frozen mages grew more and more powerful and she fed on it like a hungry leech feeds on blood.

"Sleeper, wake" the Primarch breathed "what in the name of all that's holy are you?!"

The girl turned towards him. With a gentle wave of her hand she dismissed the four Confessors.

The mages, with the grimace of voiceless scream, *decayed*, turned into nothingness in a second.

Their bodies turned into dust, as they crumbled, like broken sand castles kicked by a child.

The girl smiled at the Primarch, her overwhelming will hitting him like an halberd hits a man-at-arms.

"Who are you?" the Primarch resisted. All his power, every prayer he ever uttered was poured into the counter-attack he mounted against this creature of damnation.

And the redhead grinned at him.

"I am the shadow in the corner of your eye" she whispered, her will hammered down on the Primarch. The mosaic stones around the priest broke one by one, being unable to bear the clash of the two great wills. "I am the knowledge of her never wanting you. I am the wish for it to stop once and for all. I am autumn, I am leaves falling, I am your hair turning grey."

The marble stone altar of the Gods of Order ruptured and then sparked into unnatural flames.

The Primarch stepped backward. He was losing this battle of willpower, he knew defeat came in the face of this powerful, evil creature.

"Are you… are you a demon?" he panted.

"I am the very day of everyman's death" she continued to smile "I am the name you call for with your last breath. I am everything you didn't do, I am all you couldn't get. And I am decay you find in the graves."

Fire was bursting up from everywhere around them – cold stone, glass and the very essence of reality was burning around them. And then the Primarch realised who he was dealing with.

"You will not have this city" he shouted, his will a force hacking, slashing around him, chips of stone flung in every direction. "You are not returning, you are banished for all eternity by Shi'Ara and the Gods of Order. You are nothing more than a Howling in the Dreams of the Sleeper…"

Her grin became fierce.

"Amen" she muttered, her will crushing stone into dust under them in the depths of a mile.

"Just…" the Primarch was losing his strength. He clenched his hands into fists, as he fell to his knees. "Begone, monster!"

"Say it!" she grinned, stepping forward, smelling her victory. "Say my name!"

"Eradicata" he breathed hard, collecting the final strains of his power against a fallen god. "Lady of Decay and Despair… begone!"

"Old Gods" she touched his face with surprising gentleness "are never gone, Primarch Asturius. We merely slumber."

There was just no way he could beat an Old God, no matter what he knew about magic.

With the very last flicker of his power he sent out a rallying call, a call for help. He knew he was already dead, but Corona still had time. The city could still be saved. If enough of his brothers hear his warning and hurry here… thousands will survive.

Even if he doesn't.

"Old Gods" he rasped "may slumber… because we are awake… and will never surrender our world to you without a fight!"

"We wouldn't have it any other way" she laughed.

Enraged, the Primarch found a power deep in himself, a strength he wasn't even aware of. He unleashed all his power upon the dark creature. Her eyes were clouded with surprise, she didn't expect any resistance.

The magic of the Primarch slid all across her mental shield. The power of the two, the priest of Order and the Old God crossed each other and exploded in a furious storm.

The millennia-old grand temple of the Catechumenate was instantly vaporised, the thundering sound striking Corona as a hammer strikes the anvil, breaking windows and glasses all around the district.

Boulders of stone fell upon the city as rain falls on a stormy day. The Catechumenate, the largest building in the province, the centre of religion and magic was no more.

And amidst all the destruction, dust and ruins, a fragile, beautiful silhouette stood. Her features noble and savage at the same time, she reached to her right arm, looking for a specific bracelet.

One she couldn't find.

Chapter 6: Business

Getting to meet Shadow wasn't just hard.

It was also a very, very long process.

The meeting place was a long abandoned manufacture of war equipment, the huge hall containing more than a hundred of work stations. Maaz worked in such places before all of them closed in the Ruffian District, and hated them with all his heart.

Yet, they were still better than thievery.

He was still waiting when the great cloud of dust appeared above the Isterion Quarter, the district of the rich. Some beggars clapped their hands on the streets.

"The Gods have made judgement! The rich must suffer!"

Maaz didn't believe that for a split second. He never thought the rich deserve punishment – he just wanted to join them one day, and only a fool wanted bad things to happen to himself.

But right now even that dream was far away. He just wanted to join his sister in the monastery of the healers, and he wished the Gods of Order would grant him this wish.

He had no idea that other gods were at work here, ancient powers of infinite destruction who still longed for usurping the world, the incarnation of the dream they were the first witnesses to.

At dusk, Maaz was called for by someone who entered the room as a shadow.

Maaz was led into a dark room bereft of all pleasantries. In the nightly darkness he only saw a small table with a few bottles of booze on it.

And there was a man. A man of unimaginable old age. He must have been more than fifty! Maaz only knew a handful of people who were so old. The man was bald and even though his face and hands betrayed him to be old, his eyes were young as they shined in the candlelight.

"I reckon you are Maaz" he smiled wryly.

"My... lord... Shadow..."

"Chill, mate, I'm not Shadow" the old man laughed with a dry sound "but what I see, Shadow sees and what I hear, Shadow hears. So, out with it, what do you want?"

"I… I want to repay him and leave the city."

Shadow's man was clearly amused. At least, Maser reckoned he might be, since his laughter filled the room.

"You must have tried the booze for the first time in your life, kid!" the man emphasised each and every word. "There. Is. No. Paying. Back."

"But there is."

"Not for you, no fucking way. You owe Shadow a lot, I've seen the Charter. Now get out of here."

"But I can repay him."

"There's just no way…"

He suddenly fell silent as a shadow came alive next to him. Whether the shade was standing right next to him the whole time or it just got there, Maaz never knew.

"Enough, Gilbert. The kid's serious. I will hear him."

It was Shadow, the real one, his voice no more than a muffled whisper. He had a hood on, but his face was visible — there was nothing extraordinary about him, a man in his thirties with the face of a commoner.

Yet, he was Shadow. The Shadow, the lord of the Ruffian District.

The Lord of Maaz.

Whose attention suddenly turned to the boy.

"So, Maazer, one of my best, why have you come to me?"

"Lord Shadow… I… came to repay my debt to you."

"That is a generous proposal, my young friend, but I'm afraid you don't have what you offer to give me. You owe me *a lot*."

"But…"

"But money is just a technicality. One can offer so much more."

The king of thieves stepped to a window and looked out at the unusually dark sky.

"I leave Corona this very night." Maaz went on. "That's why I came to you."

"You are not leaving Corona."

"But my sister…"

"It wasn't an order, Maaz. You *cannot* leave the city." He laughed, seeing the confused face of the boy. "You got to love Corona and her majestic, tightly locked gates! You know, those black clouds… aren't really clouds. They're smoke. The Isterion Quarter is in turmoil. Reports are conflicting, but all agree that the Catechumenate is no more, it was swallowed by some fireball, along with the Primarch himself.

"But… that's impossible…"

"Said to boy who wishes to repay Shadow his money. *That's* impossible. Anyway, seems like Corona's end is close. Already battlemages are swarming into the city to hunt down the thing that did this. We must hide and only emerge after they are gone. And I still fear: without the pilgrims, Corona will wither. And we will decay with her. So we must take drastic measures… like accepting repayment from even our best."

He smiled at Maaz.

"Show me what you want to repay me with."

Maaz pulled the golden bracelet from his pocket and threw it to the master thief. Shadow caught it and examined it.

"Wait a minute…" horror washed through his face "I'm not accepting this."

He tossed the bracelet back to Maaz.

"Why not? It is real, it's made of gold… so why not?"

"Because it's your ginger girlfriend's, that's why! You might not have heard, but it actually *is* her the damned battlemages are looking for. It was her who destroyed the Catechumenate and set most of the palaces on fire."

"Her?…"

"Yes, her. Are you always so dumb?"

"No… sir."

"The gates are closed. Not even high ranking guards can pass and leave the city. So I guess that even if I accepted you proposal, which is absolutely out of the question, that leaves you in the city."

"But my sister was brought into the monastery, in the hills! I need to get to her!"

"Tell that to the gate guards tomorrow." Shadow smiled joylessly. "This city has been a mother to me. To see her fall like this… there is even rumour of a plague, you know? Something foul in the Isterion Quarter. All is happening so quickly! My father and his father before him… they lived their lives, and knew that Corona will be there for their offspring. It is as if something dark was secretly watching the city, and now it struck like lightning."

Silence fell. Maaz didn't know what to say.

"You will repay me, all right" Shadow sighed. "But not necessarily how you imagined it."

Then Maaz heard it, the sound he was trained to notice.

"No… you didn't…"

The soft creaking of padded leather.

"You... you..."

The harsh clinging of metal on metal, as the scabbard hits the belt.

Shadow was smiling.

"Honest business" he explained. "You sell something you own. And I do own you, Maazer. I mean, did. There was a buyer I couldn't decline."

"But... the Charter says... thieves do not sell each other out!"

"As I said... business."

Thudding of feet could be heard from the outside room.

A tear ran down Maazer's face.

"I believed in you" he said. "I... go to hell!"

He didn't think for an instant. As the door opened and the first guardsman appeared, he ran and jumped through the window, passing by the shocked Shadow.

It was so obvious! Why else would Shadow want to meet him in a room that's high up? And why wouldn't the guard come after him, if the battlemages put the redhead on their most wanted list? She *went over* to him after all, what's more, she spoke to him and gave him something.

Maaz saw the ground coming towards him with alarming speed. He tried to ease his fall by rolling, but wasn't entirely successful, as pain struck into both his arms and legs.

He jumped up and ran, in case a guard finds the courage to jump as well. He wasn't afraid of them, he could lose a soldier like that anytime – in broad daylight too. And now night has come.

With a terrible, burned stench all over. Why hasn't he noticed?

He reached the Rat's Rot without anyone even tailing him.

The usual folk sat around the tables, he knew each and every one of them by name, as he scurried into the inside room only a select few knew about. He needed to think. He sat down in a dark corner, where nobody ever disturbed him.

Going back to the healer was not an option – not anymore. They couldn't leave. Maaz knew for a fact that there were no other ways out of Corona. The walls were high and well-guarded, and on the other side, after crossing the burning Isterion Quarter, there was the ocean – after five hundred feet of free-fall. Maaz was apparently good with three storeys of height, but five hundred feet sounded too much. Although he always wanted to see the ocean, which was only a few miles away from the place he lived his life, he didn't plan to do it like this.

A flicker in the wind, a burst of colours, a smile on the Sleepers face.

Somebody grabbed and raised him from his seat.

He looked into the beautiful bluish-green eyes which sat in a face that was alike to the Sleeper's sky.

"You little rat" the redhead growled "Where the hell is my bracelet?!"

Chapter 7: Howling

"Put me down first!" Maazer's anger quickly vanished as he looked into her eyes. "Please…"

She let out a deep breath and put her down, her many bracelets clinging with the movement.

"Give it back. Now."

"All right, all right. Here."

He wanted to try to bribe one of the guards at the gate the next day, but if Shadow was telling the truth and that was one sin he never committed, it would have been in vain. So he pulled out the bracelet and gave it to the girl.

But a shadow fell on her face again.

"Where is the jewel?" she demanded. "There was a jewel embedded into this. Where is it?"

She tossed the item back to Maaz. The stone was indeed missing. Which could only mean one thing.

"Shadow" the boy sighed "that sneaky bastard!... He took it out while examining the bracelet."

The girl looked terrified a surprising emotion for someone who reportedly blew up half the rich people's district.

"Get it back" she quickly regained her composure. "I need that stone!"

"I understand it's beautiful, but…"

"You don't understand a thing! Where is this Shadow person?"

"I don't know. Nobody does. And those who know don't talk about it."

"I rephrase my request, then."

She was so beautiful! Her freckles, her eyes, her angrily pursed lips…

"You might have heard of the plague in the district of palaces?"

"Yes, I have."

"That plague is my doing. The body of the victim is burning up from the inside, their intestines turn into a bloody ooze, which they eventually vomit up."

"Sleeper, could you spare me the details? I am a man of visual intelligence."

"You and intelligence in one sentence? That would be a mistake, I guess... Anyway. My offer is as follows: get me that stone back until dawn. If you don't, this whole city will rot alive. If you do, only the Istarion Quarter people will. Do we have a deal?"

"Who are you?" Maaz whispered. He was scared of his wits – because he believed her. However frightening and mad it seemed, he could feel she's telling the truth.

"I am just a howling in the wind of the Dreams" She answered "And believe me, if I say so, that even if I weaken when I'm deprived of my stone, I will have the power to make this city rot."

Maaz didn't understand. He didn't want to.

"You have until dawn. People are already dying." The girl yawned. "I will be here. This body is... so weak."

She sat down with her back against the wall, apparently in hope of a nap, her long, red braids all over her shoulders.

Maaz sighed and scurried off, already feeling the weight of what he suspected would be the longest night of his life.

He had to get out of this city. He had no intention to die here.

So he needed the healer after all.

Chapter 8: Secrets

Emerich was eating his supper when they brought the boy to him.

He looked even more weathered than before, in the morning.

"It's not midnight yet" the healer gestured for him to sit down.

"I know, I know, I'm sorry" Maaz sat down and examined the roast chicken wishfully. "It's just that... we have to leave. Now."

"What? Why?"

Maaz ignored the questions completely.

"Listen. The city is in total lockdown, but you can get us out of here. Not even the gate guards would stand in the way of a healer!"

"Why the sudden hurry?"

"And you could give me a robe. I give it back, after we got to the monastery of course! You could say I'm your apprentice. And I swear I will be your apprentice, for the rest of my life, just let's do this while she's asleep!"

The old man's eyes narrowed. Maaz realised he gave just gave away too much.

"She? What she?"

"The redhead. She's in the district."

"And we should run away like children while she's asleep because...?"

Maaz sighed. He desperately needed the help of this man. He had to be honest with him.

"She's dangerous. I swear, she's not even human! She herself said so. Something from the Catechisms."

"Which one?"

"I don't know. I only saw preachers on the most sacred holidays. I never left the Ruffian District in my life."

"What did she say exactly?" Emerich asked and raised his mug to drink some cold herbal tea.

"Howling, she said she's howling in the wind, whatever that means."

Emerich put down his cup. He lost his appetite and he felt he couldn't swallow tea either.

"You spoke to her?"

"Yes, she came to me and told me to get her bracelet back..."

"*Get her bracelet back?* From where?"

"Ehm... from somebody who stole it."

"And why would she come to you to ask to retrieve it? You're not a city guard!"

"Well..."

"I don't suppose it's because you made friends in the morning."

Maaz remained silent. He didn't know what to say.

Emerich sighed.

"You have to be honest with me. I cannot help you otherwise."

"My sister, Rini" Maaz began, shame burning his face red. "We... work together. One of us plays the beggar, and..."

"And the other approaches those driven by their goodwill and steals their purses while they toss some coins for the beggar." The old man nodded. "Nothing ever changes."

"I'm sorry?"

"Go on."

"This morning was so dull; she was on edge and chose to steal from the redhead."

"Wait. Let me get this straight. Your sister decided to dodge four battlemages and steal from someone who calls herself Howling."

"Yes."

"Forgive me for saying, but I don't think your sister's one of Corona's brightest."

"I know, we made terrible mistakes...what is this Howling-thing anyway?"

"Ages ago the goddess Shi'Ara led an army of light against the dark elder gods that existed before. They fought and destroyed these nightmares, turning them into mere echoes, a Howling in the dream.

Some people, who are sensitive enough sometimes get under the control of the lesser nightmares, who escaped the final battle of the Celestial War. The Primarchs of the Catechumenate can banish these beings, thus saving the human they inhabit. Probably that's why your girl friend was brought to Corona in the first place."

"She's not my friend."

"I know, sorry. There is one thing I don't understand, though. What is she doing here? The spirit should have been exorcised from her body hours ago."

"Sha... ehm... someone told me she killed the Primarch and destroyed the Catechumenate. That's why the city is in lockdown, there is no passing from a district to another either."

Emerich seemed troubled.

"That's what the fuss is about," he murmured. "More than forty Confessors have arrived in the city, according to the latest estimates provided by my order."

"Your order?" Maaz laughed out. "Since when does the healing order of Shi'Ara track the battlemages?"

"It does not." The old man snapped. "We both have our secrets."

"The difference between us is" Maaz grinned broadly "that I can see through you, and you don't see through me."

"Pardon me?"

"You know the methods used by thieves well, yet you also have knowledge of the highest order: knowledge about the workings of the battlemages. This means two things: you come from low and strive for greatness. That is why you know both worlds so well."

"You speak in riddles. Everyone comes from low and wants to achieve greatness."

"Then what about this: you were once a little bastard thief like me, that's the reason for your sympathy towards me and my sister, that's why you know the criminal world. Yet you wanted to be somebody, so you have approached Sh'i Ara. You failed though, that's why you're just a healer and not one of the Lighwardens with their shining armour and holy swords. And you have not given up, so you must be part of an order of spies working for the Lightwardens. Am I correct?"

The old man eyed him grimly.

"I should kill you already for knowing about all this," he said.

"But you will not."

"No, I will not. Exactly because of my sympathy towards you and your sister. Exactly for the reason you mentioned."

"Will you help me leave the city, then?"

"Yes. But you will give me something in return."

"Like what? I have nothing."

"You know more about the redhead than anyone. Tell me. What else did she say to you?"

"She said she unleashed some sort of plague upon Corona, and if I fail to deliver a stone for her, everyone will die, rotting alive."

"Stone? What stone?"

"It was embedded into this bracelet."

The healer examined the carefully crafted, golden piece.

"This is ordinary gold" he said, frowning. "Nothing special about it."

"She wasn't interested in getting the bracelet back. She wanted the stone."

"Yes. The stone... what did it look like?"

"Well, I didn't get a very good look..."

"Come on, boy! It's not like I'm going to give extra handouts here!"

"A supper would do."

"You'll eat, then. But first tell me about that jewel!"

"It was blue. A blue cube, its form reminded me of building blocks I had as a child. And it had very small, very intricate symbols etched into its sides."

Now the monk grew anxious. He jumped up, hurried out with a word and returned shortly with a very old, heavy book. By the time he came back, Maaz was halfway done with his roast chicken and bread.

He didn't mind, he did not even notice.

"I should have known when you mentioned the plague" he said. "Look at these symbols! Could these have been on the sides of the stone?"

Maaz looked at the series of six carvings drawn on the yellow pages.

"Definitely" he said, his mouth will with delicious meat. "Yeah, these were the ones."

"You said you didn't have a good look."

"And you said you're a simple healer. We square?"

"Yes. Yes, I think so." His expression grew troubled.

"What?" Maaz inquired.

"These are the symbols of an ancient deity, a goddess our ancestors used to adore when they were living in caves and hunting for their sole survival every day."

"What kind of goddess?"

"One before the Gods of Order came and defeated them in the Celestial War. She was an Old God, killed by Shi'Ara, our goddess of healing herself."

"Apparently, that's not how it happened. I mean, the killing part."

"Yes, it would seem so. Her name is Eradicata, the Lady of Decay and Despair." He showed an illustration of the book to Maaz. It was a painting of a beautiful lady in a long, tight black dress, the six symbols drawn around her face. Her eyes were the eyes of an unloving doll – or even more like the eyes of a corpse. "She was always so subtle, so ethereal, that she used binding stones, jewels of power to bind her physical form into our world. I guess that's what she uses that girl for

"This is all very interesting" Maaz stood up from the table. "But she said that everyone in the city will catch the plague and die, if I don't return the stone to her."

"Let's get that stone then!" Emerich nodded, and closed the book. "Until we figure out how to deal with her, we must get it back to her to avoid further deaths."

"No, you old moron, let's get the hell out of Corona!" Maaz sighed. "We don't make deals with fallen gods, or whatever this thing is, we run away from them. Let the battlemages deal with her!"

"We cannot do that. We must trick her somehow."

"For that you should trick Shadow to give it back first. Which is already impossible. And after that you'll have to trick a goddess, who found me with surprising ease not long ago in one of the biggest cities in the world."

"You can arrange a meeting with this Shadow. I'll negotiate to get the stone back."

"Leave me out of this. It is your failed life you want to put right. I'm not dying for that!"

"Maaz, we could be heroes!"

"It isn't about me being a hero, it's about you becoming a Lightwarden!"

"It's not about me becoming anything" Emerich shrugged, and it was his turn to grin. "Also, there are seven of the city guards in the room next to us, having supper with our prior. It only takes for me to raise my voice, and you are done for. Don't you think I would know about the bounty on your head?"

"You... you are blackmailing a child!"

"No. I am blackmailing a known, wanted criminal. Who's just given a chance to prove he's not a worthless coward."

"A worthless coward with a duty to remain alive so I can provide for my sister!"

"Your sister has nothing to do with this. Admit it, you just want to run away. Do the good thing, Maaz!"

"Oh, no. You're not dragging me into this."

"Fine. Shall I invite those fine gentlemen over?"

Maaz shook his head. It was pointless. He could not get out of the city without this man anyway.

"Why me?" He let out a deep breath. "Why do this to *me?*"

"I saw you being touched by the Sleeper, Maaz. You were sitting there not like a beggar, but like a saint, engulfed in the light of his god. You wear the Sleeper's smile like others wear their clothes, my boy."

"Yeeeeeeeah, right."

"You don't have to believe me, but look into your heart! You did feel something, didn't you?"

As a matter of fact, he did. He felt the exact same feeling Emerich just described.

And he found a previously unknown source of willpower in his heart.

"If we're doing this," he raised his finger "we will do it my way."

"Understood."

Chapter 9: My City

Shadow,

I have come to the only logical conclusion. I cannot outrun you. I cannot hide. I cannot outsmart you. Listen, I just want my sister to be happy. Send her one tenth of the bounty you'll receive for me, and I'll be content to surrender myself into your custody. Meet me at the plaza before the Rat's Rot at exactly midnight.

Know that I made the same offer to a guard officer. I don't care, who, but somebody must take care of my sister when I am no more.

Maaz

Shadow was no fool. When Old Haggard came to him with the message, first he thought it's a trap. But then he realised, the boy lacks the resources and cunning to set a trap like that. He couldn't have gone to the guard to set Shadow up – the criminal overlord had a much lower bounty than Maaz right now.

Insulting, but that's how things were.

He established the perimeter the same way his father and grandfather did: thirteen assassins placed in secure locations, with overlooks to each other and the main theatre. He stood in the middle, hiding in the shadows next to the entrance of the Rat's Rot.

Little did he know about a fallen goddess slumbering behind his back.

His plan was to catch the little bastard and get his money as soon as possible. Then get out of the city: his eyes and ears already whispered rumours of some sort of plague attacking most of the population. Thousands, tens of thousands at the same time. He suspected magic – and, well, since a building the size of a smaller district just went up in smokes, he might have been right.

He wanted out. Now. This day was a day from hell.

Maaz didn't arrive till midnight, a bell was striking the Sleeper's Lullaby somewhere. It ended, and the boy still hadn't arrived.

He thought of money.

Thinking of money usually cleared his head, the greater the sum the better. But he couldn't get rid of his feelings right now. Sadness over losing Corona and anger, burning wrath.

He hated when he was ripped of something he once had.

Maazer suddenly dropped out of the nightly dark. He was good, very good, Shadow admitted. Good enough to become the next Shadow, should he survive the coming days.

He stepped forward.

"Maazer, my young friend!" He greeted him with a sarcastic bow. "It's good to see youth still has a tendency to use reason."

"Call off your men" Maazer whispered to him. "Now."

"What are you..."

"I know that you have thirteen assassins around. That's how it has always been in this city. Call them off, or they die."

"What are you..."

But then it had already happened. Thirteen men and women in healers' robes straightened up at the spots where Shadow has put his agents before. Blades in their hands.

Blood dipping on the ground.

The criminal overlord eyed Maaz angrily.

"A dozen of *healers* butchered my best men. Care to tell me what the bloody hell this means?"

"Shadow, hear me out…"

But the man already drew his shortsword and lunged forward with a vicious strike. Maaz jumped sideways, and ducked the cut that aimed for his throat.

The master thief changed the course of his sword, narrowly missing the boy with his next thrust.

"Shadow, listen…"

The man growled, his next swipe with the blade cutting a narrow red line on his opponent's forehead.

Maaz knew what was coming. Nobody crosses Shadow. Those, who did, died.

But those, who died didn't have a squad of Lightwarden spies on their side.

Emerich came up behind him and with a single blow to his neck sent Shadow to the ground, unconscious, his spies dissolved into thin air.

"One day we'll regret this" Maaz told him solemnly.

"Before or after we become heroes? Come on, find that stone."

Maaz began to search through Shadow's many pockets. Empty, all of them.

"Come on, where is that stupid stone?" Maaz murmured.

"Sorry, but did I hear you say 'stone'?"

The blood froze in Maazer's veins.

The beautiful redhead stood in the door of the Rat's Rot. She was rubbing her eyes wearily as she stepped out, human in every inch.

Except for her bare feet, which were absolutely clean in spite of all the muck she was walking through.

"This man had it" Maaz said in a sorrowful voice, slapping Shadow in the face to wake him. The man carefully opened one of his eyes. "He had it, I swear, but now he doesn't!"

The irritation of the girl was clearly visible.

"I need that bloody stone, don't you see?" She yelled, as she gave free way to her anguish. "Without that stone, I will wither, this body is so weak!"

"So that stone binds you to your body?" Maaz asked innocently. Emerich watched him in shock, but since the boy planned a successful attack on the criminal king of the whole province, he didn't intervene.

"Damn well it does!" She shouted, and strode forward. "Let me see that guy!"

"Useless. He's dead and he doesn't have the stone" Maaz sighed.

The girl's despair grew and grew. She tore at her hair.

"Isn't it possible for you to find that stone with your power?" Maaz asked, as if trying to help.

"My power is weakening without that stone touching my skin, you little shit!" She spat out. "I don't care how, but get me that stone, whatever it takes, or I swear, I will spread the plague I brought here upon all of

Ollundra and every single one of the inflected will curse you with their dying breaths, Maazer!"

"But if you could blow up half the rich people's district…"

With an angry scream she held out her hands.

Her power slashed forward and hit the healer and the young thief hard. They flew across the small plaza like two little stones thrown by a child.

They broke a metal lamp-post, it broke, bringing almost complete darkness upon the small square.

"Wait, wait!" Maaz struggled to his feet, trying to calm the angry goddess. "It's not like anyone would want to break that stone! It looks too valuable, even without the bracelet…"

"Shut up!" She screamed at him, her power throwing him away again. Emerich drew a short sword, when he saw that she is coming at them, but she grabbed it by the blade and broke it to a hundred pieces by clenching her fist.

"And you… following that lying bitch" She grinned at the healer. "If your Shi'Ara really killed me in that battle… how am I here, you pitiful creature?"

"I… don't know…" He fought her power, but eventually fell on his knees.

"I tell you then. I'm here, because you cannot kill an Old God. We merely slumber, as your pathetic excuse for a god very well knew. And our dreams are running out. We are waking up. And woe to you on the day we finally come to our senses and awaken, for this world is ours!"

She walked past the healer to get to Maazer, who was trying to get up with the help of the wall of a building.

"You can't stop us from waking" She whispered.

"It was his blasted idea" Maaz pointed at the healer. "If it was just me, I'd be… well, far away."

"No problem" She got to him and smiled. "Something will end now."

"That's right, you whore."

She turned in surprise to see Shadow stand in the middle of the plaza.

The tiny stone under his ironed boot.

"That's for messing with *my* city!" He groaned and cracked the magical stone.

The girl threw her head back and let out a terrible, inhuman howl, her body shaking uncontrollably.

In the nightly darkness, something even more dark rushed out of her body through her nostrils, ears, mouth, even eyes.

Then all of a sudden she collapsed beside Maaz, the usual nocturnal darkness seemed as bright as daylight.

Shadow was still bruising the stone into a thousand pieces with his foot, just to be sure.

The healer rushed to the girl to examine her with his magic. Light connected his fingers to her forehead as he did so.

"She's alive" He said. "Alive, and herself, without any darkness again."

"Good for her" Maaz panted.

"Good fucking plan, boy" Shadow stepped over to them, and patted the boy's shoulder.

"For a moment I thought you are going to kill me."

"For a moment I thought so too. But you were too clever. Would be a shame not to exploit you later on. And you actually repaid me."

"How?..."

"You gave me the one who killed my city." Shadow looked at the girl hatefully. "And quiet elegantly, too. I think, I start to like you."

"We still have to stop the plague she started" Emerich said. "I can feel the corruption all around us. It's not spreading, but it is not fading out either."

"She gave me this in the morning" Maaz held up the silvery medallion the girl presented him with. "And it has a vial-shaped something on it."

"Those runes on it" The healer examined the necklace eagerly. "Those are Shi'Aran insignia. This may be a mighty artefact of healing!"

"But how could we use it to heal everyone in the city?" Maaz was thinking.

"Pour the contents of the vial into the river Eyron" Shadow suggested. "It runs through the whole city, and let's not think about it, but apart from pissing into it, everyone drinks from its waters."

"That seems like a good idea" the healer nodded. "Let's do that and save your city, Shadow."

Chapter 10: Ollundra Withering

Maaz gently slapped the redhead a few times.

She woke, her gaze deadly tired and tormented.

"Hey" Maaz tried to smile. It was hard with a few broken ribs, which he suspected he had. "What's your name?"

"Shiwain" The girl sat up, and looked around herself. "I… what happened?"

"The young man liberated you from the tyranny of the foul spirit" Emerich announced majestically, winking at Maaz.

"Actually it was Shadow here" the boy shrugged "But I had part in it, yes."

"Thank you for it" She smiled weakly. Maaz loved her smile.

And he noticed that her arms and feet are already dirty, as a final proof that the dark goddess left for good.

"Can you walk? I'll help you. We must get out of here. And do some more valiant heroism…" He cast a dark sideways glance at the healer.

At dawn they reached the ancient artificial canal where the Eyron entered the city. It was already fast and strong. The three of them watched Maaz take the necklace and open the little vial. He poured its contents into the river.

Emerich closed his eyes in concentration, as he was trying to determine whether it worked or not.

"Nothing changes" He muttered. "I can still feel the plague feeding on thousands!"

"Maybe it needs time" Shadow shrugged.

"Some magic needs words or songs" Shiwain chimed in. Both men looked at her in a way that she held up both arms. "Yeah, sorry, I forgot I'm the uncivilised savage *woman* in the group and so my name is *Miss Shut It.*"

"Yes, exactly" Shadow nodded. "Thank you for putting it so nicely."

"Still nothing" Emerich told them with growing despair in his voice.

Maaz opened his mouth to say some soothing words, when…

…a flicker in the wind, a burst of colours, a smile on the Sleepers face…

And a Voice entered his head. A voice filled with malice, darkness and hatred.

"Your despair is most sweet, Maazer Magnusson! That's why I chose you three. The healer with his desperate wish to do good, the master thief with the silent desperation of a rich person losing everything and you, the coward with dreams as clean as those of the Sleeper's!"

"So the vial…"

"Of course the vial is a fake. Now feel the depths of your loss! You lost everything. Your living, your home… even your sister."

"Leave Rini out of this!"

"I just *love* your desperation. I love *all* your despair. I love to drink it in."

"You blasted…"

"There is a new war coming, Maazer Magnusson. What I did in Corona will happen in every city, every town and every village. We will take more people like I took the redhead and invade every settlement. The Catechumenates are going to fall, each one of them will be swallowed by flames and despair will wash Ollundra clean. The world will wither in the unending autumn that is Eradicata. And the Old Gods will reign supreme once again! We will wake!"

"Don't be so sure. We'll have a few words to say about that."

"You? Don't be ridiculous… anyway. I lingered long enough. Have some fear for me, though."

"Fear? What kind of fear, you freak?"

"The best kind. The fear for your life."

The Voice was gone. And then Maaz knew.

A flicker of blades in the wind.

A burst of colourful flames.

And a smile on the Sleepers face who enjoys dreaming exciting, violent dreams about that little thief in Corona.

Tastes change, after all.

"You all! Halt!"

A platoon of city guard ran into the room. They had their weapons in hand: axes, short swords, some even had bows with arrows on the ready.

"Oh for f…" Shadow rolled his eyes.

"You are all under arrest" The guard captain told them. "And exactly where she told us we will find you."

"She? Who 'she'?" Maaz asked.

"Her" the captain pointed at the girl. "She told us yesterday she'll lead us to the most wanted of Corona and so she did."

"I was possessed!" The girl spread out her hands.

"Excuses, excuses" Shadow said angrily and turning his back to the soldiers he faced the others. His face was calm though, as he inclined towards the river. "Maybe you shouldn't get possessed, and then…"

And then he jumped, along with the others.

Arrows hit the quickly running river's surface as it dragged them along. They were the playthings of the Eyron.

Both banks were filled with guards, shooting arrows and throwing stones...

It was the worst ten minutes of Maazer's life. He was trying not to drown and tried to help Shiwain stay above the surface, as people were shooting arrows at him...

Oh, he feared for his life, sure. He knew the dark goddess is laughing at him, wherever she is - along with the Sleeper...

Then as he finally caught Shiwain and helped the redhead swim with the quick waves – the city suddenly disappeared from both sides, and looking down Maazer saw the ocean for the first time in his life.

It was beautiful.

And far away, but coming very quickly.

Maaz coughed again and again, until there was no more salty sea water left in his body, or so he thought. He had come ashore some miles to the south with the help of Shadow, who now helped Shiwain drag the healer to the shore.

All survived, which was a miracle in itself, although Maaz couldn't remember anything after the fall.

Now he saw Corona on the grand cliffs above the ocean, with the treacherous Eyron falling from the heights.

You could see so far! Everything was so… big here.

Even the army that surrounded Corona from the outside.

"They are not letting anyone out" Shadow said. "This must be more than a whole legion! This is a quarantine indeed."

"Corona is finished" Maaz nodded. "The vial was a fake."

"The arrows weren't" Shiwain pursed her lips angrily as she showed them the long, bloody wound on her leg.

Shadow sat down on the wet sand and watched the city wishfully.

"There is nothing we can do" Emerich said.

"Oh, but you're wrong" Maaz shook his head. "We must go."

"Where?" Shadow asked him. "The only city I own is over there, eaten by a plague, closed in by a whole army!"

"There are other cities" Maaz said. "We must warn them. The... the Old Gods are slowly waking. Every city will face the same fate, if we don't warn them! If people don't even believe in the existence of the Old Gods, how could they defeat them?"

"So you found your inner hero after all" Emerich smiled at him proudly.

"Not at all! I just much more prefer stealing goods from people in a city than from... animals in a forest." He had to think for a moment whether stealing from animals in a *forest* (which he hadn't seen before) was possible or not.

"I could invest in another city" Shadow considered for a second. "And may the Sleeper be merciful to the next Old God I meet. Next time... I will be prepared."

"And I can help with that" Shiwain offered. "My tribe still prayed to them. I know much about the Old Gods... and after what that demon whore did to me, I'm glad to assist against them."

"Let's get your sister" Emerich rose and reached a hand to Maaz. "And then find us a city we can save."

"Take" Shadow corrected him. "But yes, the effects are the same."

As they walked towards the royal road, Ollundra herself was trembling under their feet.

Trembling of anticipation of the next Celestial War – fought right here, in this withering world.

Chapter 11: Awake

Brother Arnofalle visited each sick person in the morning, checking on them, seeing whether they needed anything.

When he entered the girl's room, he found her already sitting on the edge of her bed.

"Oh, child" The healer smiled at her warmly. "Are you already awake?"

Rini looked at him with a grin, her eyes darker than night.

"Oh, yes, I am awake..."

She played with one of the many little jewel cubes with the funny symbols she tore from that redhead girl's pocket.

Of course she was awake.

The End

About the Author

Peter is a Hungarian author who worked with Craig to help develop some of the origins of the World of Ollundra as well as introducing some of the major villains. Peter has written several books in Hungarian and this will be his first story released with Composite Studios.

The Wolves' Guardian

By

Nikki Yager

Chapter 1

The main street was busy with Market Day. The one day of the week when all those who lived in the small town could sell their wares and goods to patrons. Stalls had been built side by side for over a mile. Food stalls stretched away from Angwenth to the right: one dedicated to teas, another to goat's milk, still another to corn and tomatoes. To the left were trinkets, weapons, clothing, and other odds and ends.

Voices echoed through the alleys as villagers bartered to get the best deal and sellers tried to make a profit. The chatter calmed Angwenth as she casually walked passed each booth, peering at the sales. While she stopped at a booth that sold strawberries Angwenth overheard a little girl sniffing, holding back choked sobs.

Standing in front of the next stall over, the girl was dressed in a faded blue dress that was a few sizes too big on her tiny frame. Brown hair, similar to Angwenth's shade, lay matted against the girl's head. Dirt looked as if it had been hastily wiped off her hands and face, though she remained filthy.

Angwenth, not seeing a parent with the small child, knelt next to her. "What's wrong, sweetie?"

Between the sobs the girl looked down at the ground and wiped away snot from her running nose. "Daddy took Lucky last night, but-but… he never… " She began to cry again.

A large filthy hand wrapped around the frail child's wrist and yanked her towards the owner. "Amelia! What did I tell you? Stop crying over that damn mutt. Just drop it, he ain't coming home."

Angwenth's muscles tensed at his actions, but she forced herself to take a deep breath before standing. Her eyes were steady on the man. "What did you do to him?"

He was taller than Angwenth by a few inches, but where Angwenth was trim and muscular he showed a physique defined by slothfulness. The hair had left his head years ago, along with any youth that could shine through his eyes, which looked tired and glossed over with ale.

A snarl escaped his lips. "Mind your own damn business, girl. What I do with my own is my concern."

Tiny hands pulled on the man's arm, attempting to yank him away.

Her eyes widened and her lip trembled, as her breathing became rapid and a pleading whine entered her voice as she said

"Daddy, let's go. I'm sorry. Please don't fight the nice lady."

Her father shook her off, causing her to lose her balance and tumble backwards into the booth. She landed against the shelves, toppling all the neatly packed baskets of fruit. As they fell a woman began to scream in anger but Angwenth's blood pounded in her skull tuning her out.

Angwenth grabbed the man by the collar. With an anguished cry she pulled him closer to her face. His own went pale. "You are a disgusting excuse of a human being, let alone a father! How dare you treat your child that way, you shouldn't even treat an animal that way! You need to learn how to respect those around you, or I'll teach you!"

Shoving him to the dirt onto the fallen fruit, she glared down at him. "If I see your sorry ass hurt that girl again I will gut you, do you understand me?"

Eyes wide with shock he scrambled to his feet and hurried away. Amelia offered a fearful glance to Angwenth but quickly followed her father. Angwenth closed her eyes, took in a few deep breaths, and felt her heartbeat slowing down. Once the blood had stopped pounding in her head she realized how silent the market had become.

She opened her eyes again. A hundred gawking faces surrounded her. Behind her, a lone set of hands began to clap. The rest of the townspeople glanced at each other, unsure, but soon the whole market was clapping along. Looks of fear and confusion brightened to approval and excitement. Angwenth turned on her heel to face who started this nonsense and frowned. "Oh, it's you."

An elf stood before her in a set of elegant and well-made clothes. His leggings were pressed and his white flowing shirt left little to the imagination. His whole pale porcelain body was perfectly toned, and his grey eyes resembled storming clouds. His hair was pure white, though he was still young for his race.

"At your service, Angwenth, my darling." He bowed, his arm tucked beneath him.

Angwenth's cheeks were heated but she hid her blush by looking at the ground. She could feel the eyes of the patrons still watching her every move. *I'm a fool. I need to keep that under control, and here he is, just cheering my stupidity on.* She rushed towards him, pulling his arm into hers and yanking him to follow with her. "Let's go, Grey."

He chuckled, a warm laughter that usually made all those around join with him. "Why the rush, my darling? The crowd is not done cheering for your bravery."

"It wasn't bravery, and you know it. I lost my temper." Angwenth muttered through clenched teeth.

He turned to face the crowd as Angwenth yanked him away in embarrassment, shouting to them. "You all loved her performance, no?"

The crowd cheered and kept cheering until Angwenth pulled him into an alleyway and pushed him gently against the wall.

He grinned. "See they love you?"

Angwenth groaned. Grey always loved to put on a show; being the centre of attention was where he was most comfortable. His warm and playful personality always won the crowds over. His gorgeous looks definitely helped as well. Angwenth on the other hand looked homely and messy. While she tried to remain clean, her brown hair was a rat's nest of untameable curls, and her skin was tanned from her preference of outdoor work and play.

"Grey, this is serious." Though she couldn't help but smile.

The two had met over ten years ago in school. Grey was a well-known player and flirted with all the girls. Angwenth brushed him off when he tried to flirt with her the first time. He was so confused when he was greeted with a no, his smile faltered for one of the few times since she met him. Angwenth told herself she was the only one who could keep him grounded and from thinking he could always get his way.

Of course, Grey had taken that as a challenge and continued to try to win Angwenth over. After a year or two they built an odd type of friendship that seemed to work for them.

"How much of that did you hear?" Angwenth asked him after a few moments.

"Enough to know it had to do with a little girl and Francis did something to piss you off." He let off a snicker. "Though, a lot of things tend to piss you off, huh?"

She rolled her eyes and filled him in with the details. "You know him?"

"Yes, he's Francis Tinimon. Married to the seamstress, Laura. That's was their daughter, Amelia." Grey had a tone that he knew more about them but he didn't keep going.

Angwenth raised a brow. "What does he do all day? Drink?"

Grey shrugged slightly. "The rumour is that he started drinking, as far I can tell, a few years back when he lost his job. He worked as a lumberjack, but had a few too many fist fights and ended up getting axed, no pun intended." He grinned.

She knew that his pun was intended and wondered how long he waited to use that in conversation. She sighed. "That explains his glossed over eyes. What about the missing dog Amelia was talking about? Have you heard anything about that happening elsewhere?"

With a shake of his head he patted her on the shoulder. "I have not, but for you darling, I'll ask around. See what I can dig up with my charming smile. I'll come over to your place tonight to let you know what I found. Goodbye darling."

He blew her a kiss which she dodged playfully while muttering a thankyou to him, and headed home.

Chapter 2

It was far into the night when a knocking at the door disturbed Angwenth's peace. She had time to bathe and tidy herself up before he knocked, making her feel a little better about being next to his perfectly cleaned clothes and glowing skin. She let him in, ignoring the lewd comments about her appearance.

She poured them each a cup of tea. The house was small, but worked for her. It was one room with enough space for her bed, a wooden table, a rocking chair next to a fire pit and a small kitchen area. There were four chairs, just in case her parents ate over, but they usually remained longing for dinner guests.

Grey had sat down and sipped the tea while looking around. "You need a decorator for your home, Darling. There isn't enough femininity showing in here. Hell, if I didn't know any better, I would say you were staying at a brother's home and not your own."

With a small shrug Angwenth sipped her tea. "Suits me."

He was right about the home being bare. The blanket was tan and simple, the wooden house filled with wooden furniture. There were no flowers, pictures, or paintings making it look like no one lived there. Angwenth never had an issue with the simplicity, to her this was only a roof over her head. Her true home was the forest, and the beauty of nature was her decoration.

"True, you aren't very feminine. Still, a few flowers-"

"Grey." Angwenth warned.

As he took another sip of his tea he let out a chuckle. "Don't fret darling. I did not forget my task."

Reaching into his front pocket, he slid a piece of folded paper across the table. Angwenth reached to pick it up but Grey put his hand on hers. "Now before you look at that information, I want you to promise me to keep calm and not make any rash decisions."

Anxiety filled Angwenth's chest as she forced a nod before yanking at the note. Grey didn't let up his hold on it for another moment as he gave her a pondering look. Sighing, he released his grip and Angwenth opened the sheet. Two words and a location were written on the paper and Angwenth growled under her breath as she read:

Dog fights. Evanui' Edra.

She slammed her hands into the table, the paper ripping beneath her sweating palms. Her face scrunched up in disgust. "That despicable, horrible tiny man! How dare he do something so... so terrible to a dog!"

She hadn't seen Grey stand up yet he attempted to grab her shoulders. When his fingers touched her she yanked back, having to stop herself from punching his face. Grey was talking, or at least she could see his lips moving. Closing her eyes she shook her head, casting the anger aside. Grey's words started to come through as he was repeating her name.

"I'm fine. I'm fine." She muttered, though her tense muscles said otherwise.

His arms crossed over his chest. "You are losing your temper more often lately."

"I have it under control!" She snapped. Taking a deep breath she muttered. "I have it under control." Though she wasn't sure.

The bloodline on her father's side had always had a horrible temper. Anger would flare and take over. Their blood would seem to boil, their hearts race, as the rage took over and made sure whatever angered the host would be their main concern until it was taken care of. At first Angwenth only lost her temper when something dangerous happened or when someone's life was in jeopardy. Now it was at least once a day. Today? Twice.

If Grey caught her bluff he didn't push her. He was sitting again, sipping at his tea like nothing had happened. "You know you shouldn't go out there. It's dangerous." He sipped his drink again. "Plus, it's dirty."

Angwenth shrugged and didn't meet his eyes. "I've been out there before, there isn't anything I can't handle."

"This is different and you know it. You're upset, and you have no idea where their camp is located. Evanui' Edra is the worst forest to go in throughout all of Evanui' Austri." Grey's voice was edged with fear.

He was right, though Angwenth would never admit it out loud. Evanui' Austri's lush forests were beautiful and calm from a distance but inside lurked dangers that some men didn't even see in their nightmares. Of the three forests, Evanui' Edra, Evanui' Hild and Evanui' Therea, Edra was the most dangerous and had the most known deaths to date. That had yet to stop her from going into the forest to have freedom and be away from the people in her village.

She didn't admit this to Grey either. "I can handle it."

With a soft sigh he nodded, probably realizing there was no hope in arguing with her. "You get your stubbornness from your dad, I'm sure." Then he placed his cup on the table. "If you're going to be stupid enough to go through with this, you might as well have a plan. So, what is it?"

Sighing Angwenth plopped into the chair. "I need to stop it. Destroy it. Figure out who's running the dog fights and bring it to an end."

Grey nodded. "And how do you plan on," he used air quotes, "stopping it?"

"Find them and kick their asses. Simple." She stated as if it was obvious.

"What would that accomplish?" He asked.

Angwenth sighed. "They'd stop."

He shook his head. "No, they would be more sneaky. You need more information Darling."

With a groan she ran her fingers through her untamed hair. "You're right." It tasted bad in her mouth to say it out loud. "Maybe I can go search around. See what I learn, then make a plan."

She was greeted with a smile. "Fantastic idea Darling! Would you like company?"

Angwenth gave him a smirk and raised a brow. "You want to go in the forest? Weren't you just telling me how dangerous," she let out a soft chuckle. "and dirty it is?"

Offering a warm smile he shrugged his shoulder. "I knew you would refuse either way. All I have to gain is the joy of your company."

With a shake of her head. "Well thank you for the offer but I must decline. I need to do this on my own."

Chapter 3

The forest was eerily quiet. It was still dark out, the only animals awake seemed to be the owls. Angwenth had decided to come out to the forest tonight, since sleep was being fickle and refused to stay long enough to do any good. Whenever she grew tired her thoughts wandered back to the note making her blood boil and her heart race. It was worse than having a cup of coffee. She was wearing a path in the wooden floor pacing all night. She had to get out and do something.

Fresh trees and morning dew filled the air, calming Angwenth down as she walked as quiet as she could along the forest path. Despite the multiple warnings to never go in the forest, and the dangerous beasts, Angwenth loved the forest. She would come out here whenever she got a chance, in hopes of just a brief time of no people, no talking, and no noise. The darkness pressed in on her, but Angwenth followed a familiar path for now and had no fears of getting lost.

Her anger level was dangerously high. Any higher and she'd lose control, again. She wouldn't make rational decisions or find anything useful if that happened. She had time before dawn either way, no point searching in the dark and a light source would only draw attention from the wild life. Angwenth wanted to make it to her little home away from home and wait for morning's light, hoping that being in the midst of the forest before those in charge of the dog fights even woke would give her an advantage. Once there was some natural light she could search for clues without being caught. At least that was the plan.

    Angwenth had taken her time to reach her destination, wanting to soak in the silence before having to get back to work. When she had reached the familiar clearing the moon was starting to hide from view. She glanced at the moss-covered rock in front of her, finding the worn path where she usually walked, and followed it up to the top. At the highest point it plateaued for a few feet, providing a perfect place to sit, rest, and enjoy the world around her. This was where Angwenth retreated to get time away from the busy life of the village, or away from her nagging mother about why she didn't have a husband yet. No one knew about this spot, not even Grey. Though Grey would never come into the forest if he could help it, Phadera forbid he got dirty.

She smiled as she sat down and glanced over the edge. The sun was starting to rise, the light dancing across the trees and hitting the flowers just right. The field under the ledge started to shine with colours of the rainbow, as the warmth from the morning started to wake up the field. The light bounced off the dew drops, making it seem almost magical and filling Angwenth with happiness as she took a deep breath of fresh air. While all the creatures slept the forest almost seemed peaceful.

It took her a few moments to pull herself away from the sight, but slowly she pushed herself off the floor. She walked away from her love and towards the northern part of the forest. She was assuming that the men would want to stay hidden but still near the edge of the forest. There was no way a man like the coward from the market would stray too far into any of the forests, let alone Evanui' Edra. Her spot wasn't far from the edge, but had a few tricky manoeuvres to reach it safely, usually avoiding any visitors.

Angwenth headed back towards the edge, following it north. The light helped her as she stepped around trees, over roots, and avoided possible injury-inducing obstacles. She kept her eyes on the ground, looking for signs of humans or beasts in the forest.

After walking for a little while she ducked through a bush and took a step forward. Her eyes landed on the back of a greenish skinned beast that stood over eight feet high. Its back was bare, and it wore a tattered pair of pants that would fit Angwenth four times in one leg. Angwenth froze. *Troll.* The beast was faced away, his giant three fingered hands wrapping around a tree and shaking it violently. Small fruit fell from the tree, a few hitting the creature on the head though the troll seemed to ignore them, smile, and shake the tree again.

Trolls weren't smart but from personal experience Angwenth knew they were quick to explode with anger. *Sounds familiar. Maybe I'm part troll.* Little things could trigger their anger, and startling them was one of those triggers. Angwenth took a step back, hoping to escape before it caught scent of her. As her foot slipped back, it landed on a branch, and before she could stop her weight from pushing all the way down a loud snap echoed throughout the forest.

The troll paused, tilting it's head to lift an ear up to the sky. When the sound faded, the troll took a deep whiff of the air and his confused look shifted into a grin.

"Human?" His voice was deep. The forest floor vibrated with the sound.

He sniffed the air again, then cheered gleefully. "Human!" In his thick accent, the word came out 'Who-man.'

It turned around but Angwenth had already ducked behind a tree. She was covered, but it wouldn't take long for the troll to sniff her out. She took a deep breath and pushed herself off the tree, vaulting into a run. She heard the grunt of the troll as he found her scent. Something crashed behind her as she heard the footsteps of the troll take after her. He chanted playfully. "Human! Human!"

Her eyes darted in between the trees looking for a place to run where the troll couldn't catch her. Up was an option, but the troll easily crushed the trees in his path, and she doubted he would consider what would happen to her if he tore the tree out of the ground. She could get into a cave, but there wasn't one nearby. Running was her only choice for now.

Deep in her own thoughts of fear, Angwenth ducked as the troll grabbed a rock and chucked it at her head. It missed and slammed into a tree to her left, forcing her to sharply turn and run into a patch of trees. A pointed branch scraped painfully against her skin, just short of drawing blood. "Damn it!" she muttered.

"Human! Why you run?" He whined like a little child. *Wait! A child? He was acting like a child! Maybe I don't have to fight him.* The troll was breathing heavier as Angwenth heard it stop to pick up something else.

Trying to stay on her feet Angwenth zig-zagged back and forth, hoping to cause the troll to miss again. When a rock slammed against her back and knocked the wind from her lungs she fell forward. *Good job, zig-zag running worked out great.* Angwenth groaned as she put her hands on the ground, twitching her toes to make sure her legs were still working. They were. She pushed herself up and turned to face the troll. *This better work. Well, if it doesn't I'm dead anyways.*

Standing her ground Angwenth stared at the troll. Not easy with the height difference. The troll had a large, one-toothed smile as he looked down at her. He tapped a length of tree trunk playfully against the ground. "Human!"

Taking in a deep breath Angwenth sternly called out to him. "No! Put that down this instant!"

A confused look came over his face as his smile faltered and he looked down at the trunk. Angwenth said louder. "Put it down! Now!"

His lower lip stuck out slightly. *Is he pouting? Ha! He really is just a kid.* He chucked the trunk over to Angwenth's right. She used all her strength to not flinch as it slammed into the ground a mere foot away from her legs and kept her eyes on the troll. "Good. Now go home."

He stomped his foot in an oversized temper tantrum. "I no wanna, Human. Human play!"

Growling, as scary as she could manage, she stared him down. "Go. Home. NOW!"

He flinched back and tears started to pour into his eyes. "Human are mean! I no wanna play with you, big meanie!"

Great, you made a troll cry. A kid troll even!

Before Angwenth had a chance to say anything, the troll ran off to the west, his feet stomping in the ground, crushing anything that crossed its path. The sound of the thuds echoed throughout the forest, stirring the birds into flying away. When the stomps were far enough to no longer hear Angwenth slid down to the ground, her legs no longer able to hold her up.

She took in a few deep breaths. *Get up, you have work to do.* Her heartbeat and breathing returned to normal before she pushed herself off the ground. With a sigh she looked around to make sure there were no other beasts nearby, before heading back towards her original destination.

With a sigh she looked around to make sure there were no other beasts nearby, before heading back towards her original destination. "Need to be more careful. You're not on your game." She muttered to herself. "Oh and now you can officially say you're crazy, talking to yourself out loud." Shaking her head she walked the rest of the way in silence.

Hours passed without running into any more beasts, but Angwenth was starting to get frustrated. The peacefulness of the sunrise was gone, and the sun was starting to creep closer to the time when normal people started to wake up. She had accomplished nothing and was furious with herself for going too slow.

As she grumbled and muttered a curse she heard voices in the distance. She slipped behind a tree, peering out to find where the sound was coming from. There were two distinct voices coming from north, north east.

Angwenth shifted to keep herself hidden as the voices got louder, coming closer to where she hid. "Why the hell do we always have to go check the damn stuff? It's his job." Muttered the first his voice nasally with a whining higher pitch, maybe a kid, definitely no older than puberty.

"Oh shut up. It's too early to listen to you whine about this." A deep, low-pitched voice grumbled. "Just do your damn job, and ya won't piss off the boss." The nasally kid snorted, though it seemed more out of nerves than laughter. "What's he gonna do? Fire us. Hell, I can find another job any time I want. And it'd be a lot safer, too. There are tons of ways to die out here."

His voice was hushed and shaking slightly: a coward. Angwenth already didn't like him. At least be a man if you're going to do something illegal like this. The other man seemed to agree as he snarled. "Shut your damn mouth, kid. Get us both in trouble, and some of us have mouths to feed at home. Ya damn well know you're not going to find something that pays as well as this gig elsewhere."

They kept heading West, Angwenth moved to remain hidden behind the tree. As the voices started to carry farther she risked a peek. The two men faced away from her, walking in the same direction, bickering back and forth. On the right was the younger kid, who looked like he was barely old enough to hold a job. He was a head taller than the other man, but his face was smooth and his head was full of black curly hair. Beside him was the shorter older man with a gut that said he never missed a meal. His hairless head gleamed in the sun, as he muttered something to the boy and shoved him slightly to make him stop talking.

Angwenth wondered if they realized how loud they were being. Creatures out here would be eating it up if they caught wind. Too many creatures out here would take them as easy prey and a quick, rather filling, meal. Angwenth followed them as quietly as she could. She stepped around fallen twigs and leaves, staying just close enough to hear the conversation.

The men were about twenty feet ahead of her, and she easily followed without them noticing since they were being so loud. They continued to walk for about ten more minutes until the older man motioned to the boy to be quiet and looked up. Angwenth held her breath and hid behind the tree, before he glanced back towards where she stood.

Damn it! I was being quiet! How did he hear me with all their loud talking? After a few moments she heard the man talk again. "That trap is around here somewhere. Do you hear that whimpering?" Straining she tried to listen for the whining, but heard nothing from this far away. The boy gave out a loud cheer. "Haha! We caught one! Let's see if it has any friends with it for the games."

The other man let out a chuckle but muffled it with a hushing noise. "Keep it down. Don't want no damn company." Her chest tightened in anger as she heard that, wondering if they meant the dog fighting games. As they started to walk again she let out a breath and forced herself to slow down instead of racing in to tear them apart. Peeking around the tree she saw that they were gone, the edges of a bush fell into place where she assumed they disappeared.

Angwenth pushed away from the tree and inched her way to the bush. Through the spaces between the leaves and branches the two men were standing with their backs to her, looking down at the ground.

Now that she was closer she could hear the whimpering of a wounded animal mixed in between growls of protection. "Looks like we got ourselves a new contender for the games." The older man said. He reached down to pick something up but a loud snarl and growl were heard. A wolf.

The man jumped back, pulling his hands away from the animal. "Damn bitch." The older man muttered. "What do we do, Jack?" Mumbled the younger man as he moved nervously back and forth on his heels. "Kill it. We don't need the bitch, just her pup." Pup? Angwenth opened her eyes wide and realized what they were doing. They're trapping the mothers, killing them, and stealing their pups? For dog fights? No! Angwenth's heart began to race and when she saw the crossbow in the young boys hands it was too much. "No!" She screamed and ran through the bush.

Both men turned in surprise, the boy pointing his crossbow straight at her neck, ready to shoot. Angwenth grabbed his arm, and with her shoulder slamming into his chest, tackled him to the ground. The crossbow slid a few feet away. She pushed herself up to pin him to the ground, but he wriggled around too much for her to get a good grip. "Stop moving!" She growled. She threw a first toward his face and he dodged it. Her knuckles slammed hard into the forest floor. Growling, her face hot, she grabbed at his hair to keep him still. The older man,

Jack, stood off to the side as if paralyzed with confusion. He frowned and stepped in to help his young partner, muttering. "Damn crazies."

Angwenth felt a hand on her hair, yanking her back from the boy's face, one punch slamming into his jaw before she was pulled too far back to hit again. The kid groaned as he pushed himself up. Angwenth reached up to grab the man's hands who held her hair, but his grip was too far away. Damn long hair! I knew I needed to cut this off. "Ray, kill the dog. I'll deal with this one." Ray nodded and rubbed his rapidly bruising face as he glanced around for the crossbow.

Jack watched him, and when Angwenth noticed his attention was elsewhere, she yanked her head forward. He toppled over in surprise. Angwenth pushed up and got out of his way, as he fell to the floor. She ran towards Ray, his attention on the dog as she grabbed his arm and slammed it over her knee. A loud snap echoed against the trees, followed by Ray's high pitched scream of agony. Definitely hadn't hit puberty yet. He fell to the ground, grabbing his arm with his unbroken hand, tears running down his face. Angwenth turned back to face Jack. The handful of hair dropped from his hand, letting it fly away in the wind. "Now you're starting to piss me off." "Good, because I'm way beyond that point." She responded.

Jack ran towards her, scowling, his fist flying toward her face. Angwenth dodged, her hand grabbing the back of his shirt and pulling him off balance. As he spun around, he lost footing and landed on his back.

Angwenth towered over him, her foot pressed to his throat to keep him from standing. Wiggling under the pressure, his face showed that he was losing his air. He grabbed at her foot desperately. When his face started to turn blue Angwenth couldn't help but smile. "Now you know how those dogs feel," she hissed. "Tortured, in pain, no control."

The man's grip weakened and his hands dropped to the ground. A soft whimper broke her focus, bringing her back to reality. Angwenth looked to see a beautiful black mother wolf, white sprinkled along her nose and around her eyes. She stepped away from the dead man, and over to the animal.

Her front right paw was stuck inside a metal bear trap, the sharp edges slammed into the leg, making it useless, the paw hung limp. Behind her was a solid black pup, licking his mother's other leg in fear and protest.

As Angwenth took a step towards her, the mother wolf let out a growl. Angwenth paused, crouching down and waiting for a moment. The wolf sniffed the air and, as Angwenth grew closer, tensed. When her growling didn't continue, Angwenth took it as a sign she could continue. It took a moment for Angwenth to get her fingers in the trap and pry it open.

It released with a snap, and the wolf grabbed her pup by the neck, limping off towards the forest. Angwenth smiled as the animal glanced back at her. She closed her eyes, feeling her blood cool, her pulse settle. She let the anger fade from her system.

When she opened her eyes she saw it happen in a split second. The mother wolf, mid-stride, dropped to the ground. As a bolt flew past side of her head. She could feel the wind of the bolt rustle her hair. Jumping up and spinning on her heel, she faced Ray, his unbroken arm shaking, still aiming his crossbow at the wolf.

He frantically tried to reload the weapon his eyes never leaving Angwenth. "You killed him," he said. Angwenth glanced down at the bigger man and narrowed her eyes. She looked back up at Ray. "How many animals have you killed for your games?" Her voice was a harsh, edgy whisper. It tore through the air like the bolt. She clenched her fist to keep herself from snapping at him, worried her sudden movement would make him pull the trigger.

The young boy shook his head in disbelief. "They're just dumb animals. Should have been smarter not to get caught in the traps." Angwenth growled and took a step closer to him. His arm raised a bit higher, the crossbow pointing towards Angwenth's head.

"Don't come any closer, I will shoot you." "You're going to shoot me anyway." She said between gritted teeth, forcing herself to stand still. "Might as well take you with me." Angwenth saw the bush move behind him, but flicked her eyes back to Ray. From the corner of her eye she saw the black pup that the shewolf was carrying sneaking behind the boy. She readied herself, as the pup opened its mouth and chomped down on the boy's side. Startled, the boy lowered his weapon and went to smack away the pup.

With the crossbow no longer pointing at her, she ran towards him, and yanked the crossbow away from his hand. She tossed it away, and grabbed him by the head as she dragged him to the ground. She quickly straddled him and pulled his head up before slamming it into the ground.

"Where is your camp?" Ray looked up at her, and spit in her face in response. Angwenth slammed his head into the ground again wiping her cheek off on her shoulder in disgust. "Where?" she growled. He didn't respond. Angwenth slammed his head into the ground a few more times. "Tell me!" He laughed in defiance while blood pooled into his mouth. In a final move of anger she punched him in the face, feeling his nose crunch beneath her fist. Ray lay limp beneath her, and she stood up after a moment, kicking him in the side, and picked up the wolf pup beside him.

"Thank you," she said softly to the wolf pup. The pup licked her hand gently. Angwenth sighed and walked over to the mother wolf. She dropped into the dirt by the mother's head. The wolf raised her nose and looked up at Angwenth, whimpering softly. She placed the pup before the mom, "He's okay," she said softly, her voice a bare whisper against the air. "He saved me." The mother wolf licked her pup, before putting her nose against his rear and pushing him slightly towards Angwenth. With a nod Angwenth picked up the pup and gave a soft weak smile. "I'll keep him safe." She wasn't sure the wolf understood her, but a look of relief seemed to cross over its eyes.

The mother wolf rested her head on Angwenth's knee. Angwenth ran her fingers through her thick coat. The wolf closed her eyes. Angwenth felt her breathing slow and grow jagged. She stayed there with her until the end.

The sun was high in the sky when the black wolf let out her last breath. Angwenth sighed. "Rest now. I'll protect the little one." The wolf pup was sleeping in her lap, and Angwenth knew that now was not the time to keep hunting for the fights. She would need help locating their games, and wanted to keep the pup safe as she had promised.

Sighing, she knew she was going to need to ask Grey for help. Gently, she placed the mother's head on the ground and pushed herself up, scooping up the pup into the crook of her arm.

Chapter 4

The sun was setting by time she got home. Thankfully the beasts in the forest seemed to have hidden from the sound of the crying troll. Smart creatures. The pup had woken a few hours prior and was running at Angwenth's heels, seemingly oblivious to the loss of its mother as he chased butterflies.

When they did arrive home Angwenth sighed and sat on the bed. With a small whine, the pup scratched at her feet to get help up onto the furniture. She smiled and lifted it onto the sheets. "I need a name for you, pup. I'll think of a good one first." He tilted his head at Angwenth and barked playfully. Angwenth grinned and ruffled his ears before getting up. "I should go find Grey. I'll be back little guy." The pup whined and barked at the edge of the bed, being too high to jump off.

Angwenth smiled with a shake of her head and headed outside. It didn't take her long to find Grey. He was at the his usual hangout, the Old Mills' Tavern. The tavern was built in a sturdy grey stone on the outside, but the inside had lovely wooden arches decorating the ceilings and the walls.

There were beautiful hand carved tables with matching chairs arranged around the room. Someone had spent a lot of love and time on this tavern, and it showed in the friendships that were built inside these walls.

No one was quite sure if Old Mills was the man behind the counter, or his great grandfather. Either they all looked alike or everyone who ever entered the tavern promptly forgot if Mills the bartender, had a family.

He was a plump older man, with greying short curly hair. Mills's smile always seemed genuine and his interest was always held when anyone told him a story. He was the first to laugh at a joke, and the first to offer an ale in times of celebration or sorrow. Angwenth hadn't come very often, choosing the life of solitude over that of buddies with ale.

She had met Mills enough times throughout her life that he gave her a friendly wave and shouted out to her. "Angwenth! What brings ya to my little paradise?" Angwenth greeted him with a warm smile. "Hail Mills! I'm here to see Grey." She scanned the room and saw him in the back corner, flirting with a lady that looked too young to be in the tavern, she couldn't help but roll her eyes. Mills let out a small chuckle and nodded.

"Well, you know where to find him. Don't be a stranger, haven't seen you since you were a young'n. Do you remember?" Letting out a warm laugh of her own, she nodded respectfully. "I remember being too young to be in here, sitting on my pa's lap, listening to stories I was too young to understand." Mills ran his fingers through his curly hair and smirked.

"I kept it clean, no worries." "It wasn't you I was worried about." She glanced over at Grey again, who seemed to be making friends with the young woman's lips. "Speaking of clean. Excuse me." Angwenth walked over to the couple, pulling up a chair and making herself comfortable.

She stared pointedly at Grey and the young woman. When they were getting into the kissing, Angwenth smirked and cleared her throat. Grey jumped and spun around, blocking his face from the expected punch. "She said she was single!" Roaring in laughter, Angwenth shook her head as she watched Grey's face turn red.

The woman stood up in anger and smacked him across the cheek before storming off. Angwenth was having problems catching her breath. Grey muttered something under his breath and slumped down in his own chair. "Are you done?" It felt good to laugh after the day she'd had.

Wiping away tears that were streaming down her face, Angwenth grinned. "That was priceless." In a mocking tone, Grey muttered, "That was priceless." He rolled his eyes. "Hello to you, too." "Oh, lighten up. Consider it payback for the cheering crowd at the market." That made him smile and he shrugged. "Okay, okay. I guess we're even." He leaned forward. "I take it you have news?"

Angwenth nodded before telling him about the day. She made sure to explain that there were two men, glossing over the fact that she brutally killed them, and then brought up the pup. Grey interrupted, excited. "You got a pup? Where is the little guy?" His eyes searched behind Angwenth, as if she was hiding the pup somewhere.

She rolled her eyes. "He's at home. I left him there while I came to find you." Frowning Grey shook his head. "Well then what are we doing here? Let's go meet the little guy." His chair pushed back and scraped against the floor. Before Angwenth could get up from her own chair, Grey wrapped his arm around her arm and pulled her out of her seat. Her own chair toppled over to the floor and she attempted to pick it up, but Grey was already pulling her towards the door before she could right the furniture.

"Sorry, Mills!" she called out as the door closed to the tavern. It wasn't long before they reached her house and Grey was playing with the puppy on the floor. It chased his hands back and forth as Grey moved them across the wood. There were a few times that that the wolf nipped at his fingers and Grey yelped in pain, though it was quickly followed by a laugh.

Angwenth started pacing around the room as she told him about what happened throughout the day. The pup had stopped chasing Grey's hand and started chasing Angwenth's feet as she walked around the room. She had almost stepped on him a few times, not realizing he was there. "You just like to be under my feet, don't you?" Grey chuckled. "It's like he's your shadow."

A large grin appeared on his face as his eyes lit up. "That's it! That's the name you should use." "Shadow?" Angwenth reached down and picked up the pup. "Are you a Shadow, boy?" The pup barked and licked Angwenth's nose. She grinned. "I guess that's your new name. Welcome to the family, then, Shadow." She let him back down and went back to talking to Grey. "The guy wouldn't tell me anything. He was so stubborn!" "Reminds me of someone." Grey said under his breath. "Couldn't you find him and get him to tell you the information in different methods?" Angwenth blushed. "He's, well, he's not around to tell anyone much of anything anymore." Grey shook his head. "Surprise, surprise. You lost your temper." Angwenth shot him a look. "It doesn't matter. I'm thinking the camp wasn't far from there, though, if they were setting up traps.

They looked too scared to go too far in and they only had the one gun as a weapon." With a nod, Grey added. "They didn't seem that skilled with it either, if they couldn't kill you." "Exact-- Hey!" Angwenth turned in protest.

Chuckling he waved her off. "I kid, darling." She shook her head. "I need to get farther north. I'll try looking out there tomorrow, but I may need your help." That perked an eyebrow. "My help?" "Yes. I almost got myself killed twice today. I need your help to keep me on the lookout.

We'll stay close to the edge, and just look for the location." Angwenth added. With a sly grin, Grey added. "Plus, if we're together, it will seem like we aren't spying, we are just out for a friendly stroll. Two really good friends looking for a quiet place to keep each other company." He winked. Angwenth's face blushed before she turned away. "That wouldn't work." "Only one way to find out! If it comes up, that will be our cover story. I'll get a date with you even if it's a cover story and fake." With a groan she faced him again. "Oh, drop that whole date thing. I just need your help to find the location, then I can come back tomorrow night and take care of things, so that the fighting can end." "Whatever you say, darling." His smirk showed his true intent.

Angwenth kicked him out a little later. She had been up for almost two full days, due to this mess with the dog fights. Originally she had wanted to go straight out to find the hunting grounds, but a curled-up Shadow on her lap caused her to realize how tired she was and changed her mind. Shifting her position, Angwenth climbed into bed, Shadow curling up behind her legs as she slept soundly.

Knowing her way, Angwenth found the camp again rather quickly, though she hid behind a different bush than the last time. From her hiding spot she could see that many of the men were not in sight, though the sound of snoring established that most of the tents were full. There were two men on guard, one was leaning up against a wall, his head leaning forward in sleep, his chest rising and falling slowly. The other, an orc, stood with his side toward her, his eyes watching the forest, alert and ready for fighting. He had to go down fast.

Biting her lip, Angwenth thought for a moment before taking any action. It would take more time to start a fire than it would to kill the lone orc. More men could be killed with a few of her arrows, while they were sleeping and confused. She nodded resolutely and headed toward the tents.

Making her way around, careful to stay out of earshot of the orc, she lit a handful of twigs using flint and steel. Pulling an oil soaked arrow out of her bag, she held it above the flame. With a brilliant yellow glow, the cloth ignited into a ball of fire. Smiling, she notched the arrow on her bow, pointed towards the closest camp, and shot the arrow.

There was no wind. The arrow shot through the sky, cleanly and silently, hitting the tent in the bottom corner. Flame flicked across the fabric, searching for more fuel. It found it, and the tent started to light up. Not wasting any time, she lit, notched, and shot the additional five arrows, all at different tents. Then she took off back to where she was before, a regular arrow already placed on her bow.

By the time she made it back to her original spot, the tents were almost completely engulfed. Startled cries of different men could be heard as she pulled back her arrow, and aimed for the head of the orc that was nearby. His attention had turned to the camp, blocking him from the sound of the shooting arrow until he turned. The arrow slammed right into his eye. Angwenth winced as he fell to the ground. She had aimed for his temple.

Go, you don't have time for this. She pushed herself off the ground and notched another arrow. Men were pushing out of the tents, though some of their screams were more agonizing. Angwenth didn't look over at them. The sleeping guard jumped up, startled and confused by the screams. Before he could see what was going on, Angwenth shot an arrow at him, but missed as it hit the shed behind him. "Damn it!" she muttered before notching another. *Only four more.*

The man looked back at the arrow, then where Angwenth stood. He pulled out his sword, though he was slower due to just waking up, and headed towards her. Angwenth shot another arrow, this time hitting him in the throat and he fell over gasping for air.

Three more. She reminded herself as she notched the bow, glancing over at the tents to see who would be the biggest threats in close range combat. The fires were growing, and starting to reach the other tents. Multiple men were out of the tents, flames licking over the scream, the sources of the agonizing screams. Other men were beating them with things, in attempts to put out the fire, but were only making it worse. There were about six or seven men already on the ground, twitching or just unmoving. About ten men were still on fire, and four were singed, but not burning. There were about ten able-bodies men, though half of them were busy, and there was about fourteen able to fight still.

Angwenth groaned. The odds were not looking good but at least she had downed at least half of them. She aimed her bow for one of the larger men who had no injuries. The bow twanged. The arrow slammed in his back, cutting off his sentence. She saw him look down at the protruding arrow through his chest, before falling down to his knees. The human he was talking to looked up directly at her. Their eyes locked.

"Shit." *Two to go.*

Notching another arrow she aimed for the man, but he dodged it. The arrow shot past him and slammed into the arm of another man, one that was already on fire. He screamed, confused, and fell to the ground. There wasn't time for Angwenth to pull out her final arrow. She dropped her bow and pulled out her sword, running into the woods so the others wouldn't get any ideas and attempt to follow.

When she turned to face the human she was greeted by a stocky, short, balding man of about her father's age. There were circles under his eyes and his clothes were covered in dirt and soot from the fires, he pulled out his sword and readied for a fight. Angwenth frowned as she looked at him. The man growled.

"Why are you doing this?" He asked angrily. "You killed a bunch of good men in there!"

Angwenth raised an eyebrow. "Good men?" She repeated. "You capture and kill innocent animals for profit. Whether to sell their meat and coats, or for your stupid games. How is that a sign of a good man?"

He hesitated. "We have to make a living."

Angwenth shook her head, anger flaring up inside. "They're innocent animals!"

The man shrugged with indifference.

With a growl, she felt her face heating up. Blood rushed throughout her body, her heart racing. Her grip tightened on the hilt of her sword, left foot stepping slightly backwards. The man must have taken it as a signal and raised his sword before running towards her. Angwenth dodged his first blow, the sword slicing thin air. He stumbled forward but quickly righted himself, turning on his heel to face Angwenth.

Angwenth held the sword in front of her, using it to block. She weaved left and right, dodging a few more attacks. As one aimed for her head, she lifted the her blade to block the steel. It slammed down with a clink. He attempted to push towards her, but she was taller. Lifting up her leg she slammed the bottom of her foot into his chest, knocking him backwards.

The weapon slid across her own sword with a loud whine of metal. Her assailant landed on his ass, the blade landing on the ground near him. Without hesitation Angwenth ran at him, slamming the blade across his lower arm. It cut through cleanly; blood covered the blade as she spun around and slammed the tip of sword into his back. With a spurting cough the man collapsed.

Not having time to think about her next move, she ran away from the body to get an advantage point. She ran toward the clearing and found herself behind the pens. A few of the men had run toward the forest, while others attended the wounded. The fires were still growing, and they were getting closer to the pens, she needed to help get the animals out or they would all die. Running towards the cages she slashed the ropes that kept the cages locked. They split apart as the sword slammed against the wood.

The noise drew attention to her. Several men stood shooting surprised looks at each other. A handful of them stood before her, a few humans scattered with elves and orcs. Most were covered in soot or had burnt clothes and hair. All of them were angry, and looking straight at her. Angwenth ha an idea that brought a smile to her face.

An orc, about two feet taller than her, took a step forward. He had a head full of red hair that contrasted against his tanned greenish coloured skin. Underneath his clothes were muscles that rippled as he tensed at her smile. "Why are ya smiling? We have you cornered. You lost!"

Angwenth couldn't help but let out an almost maniacal laughter. It seemed to piss him off more.

"Stop laughin'! You're going to pay for what you've done."

"Oh you want pay back, do you?" Angwenth grinned while still letting out choked laughs.

Wary eyes were glancing around at each other, probably wondering what Angwenth was madness was causing her to face them all head on like this. Angwenth let her grin fade as she replaced it with a ticked-off scowl. "Then have your pay back, you bastards."

Doors to the cage swung inwards, opening soundlessly. The growling and snarling of the beasts grew louder as a few of them stepped out of the cages. Ears were back, hair stood on edge across their spines, as they kept eye contact on the men who had forced them into that cage. "Now's your chance boys and girls. Go get your pay back."

Men started to take frightened steps away from the animals. One took off in a run, causing three of the dogs and wolves to chase him into the forest. There were snarls and a loud scream of agony. It died after a few minutes, but gave the rest of the wolves and pups incentive to take off. After they cleared out, Angwenth ignored the screams and ran to the other two pens. She cut the ropes loose on those as well, letting them swing open so they could join in the fun.

There was nothing else for her to do. The animals would finish off what they were doing, hopefully the pets would find their way home, and the wolves would go back to living in the wild. The fires would die down before it reached the forest and grow more. She needed to go back to Grey and get him home to take care of his broken ribs and arm.

As she walked the sun started to rise. Blood-curdling screams filled the air, but Angwenth didn't look back. Her job was done. The animals were free. Now, they could have their revenge on the people who hurt them. She smiled.

Pushing through the clearing she glanced up at the cave. Grey stood at the edge of it, leaning against the wall, holding his broken arm in his grip. He glanced around worriedly. Shadow sat at his heels looking into the forest as well. The pup saw her first, his tail wagged as he let out a soft bark before taking off towards her.

Angwenth reached down to pick up the pup, letting him jump on her chest and lick at her face. "Hello to you, too." She said, her voice exhausted.

Walking the rest of the way to the cave she saw Grey. He lit up when they locked eye contact. "You shouldn't have gone off alone."

She glanced away. "I didn't want you to get hurt."

A finger rested against her chin and lifted up her head. "I didn't want you to get hurt, either."

They locked eyes again, even when Angwenth tried to look away she got lost in his grey eyes. "I'm fine. They're dead. It's over."

"That's over." With a smile Grey leaned in.

He pushed his lips against hers. They were soft, full, and seemed to lock perfectly. Angwenth felt heat rush through her body as their skin connected. At first she tensed, but as the kiss continued, her eyes closed. He broke away first, leaving Angwenth confused. "This is just beginning."

Angwenth couldn't help but blush. Her first kiss, and it was with Grey of all people. It seemed wrong but felt right. Sighing, she let out a small smile. "We need to head back to the village. You're injured, I'm injured, and I need sleep."

Grey nodded but didn't move. "I need you to promise me something, Angwenth."

She looked at him.

"Promise me that we can give this a shot." He whispered.

Angwenth looked away. "What about the other girls?"

Grey shook his head. "I will be faithfully yours as long as we are together."

Gulping slightly she fidgeted. With a curt nod she turned to walk away. The heat on her face gave away how much she was blushing and she didn't want him to see.

If he saw, he didn't say. Grey followed as they headed towards the village. The sun was in the sky, the howls of wolves could be heard from far away, the screams had stopped. A breeze brushed against her cheek and hair. Angwenth took it as a sign that Adruna was thanking her for saving the life of the forest creatures. With a nod, Angwenth kept walking in silence.

They reached the village around noon, the walk taking longer with their injuries. Angwenth lead them to her parent's house, knowing her mother would make a fuss but would take care of everything that needed to be done. Exhaustion was barely holding off as she knocked on the door.

A woman in her late fifties with white frizzy hair, matching Angwenth's own hair, answered the door. She stood a foot and a half shorter than Angwenth, who got most of her height for her father, and looked up at the two of them with sparkling green eyes. "Angwenth! Dear, what a surprise."

"Hello, Mother. We need your help." She signalled to Grey's arm and acknowledgement crossed the elder woman's face.

"Well if it isn't Mr. Grey Holst, how have you been?"

"Doing pretty well, minus the broken arm and ribs, Mrs. Longbriar." Grey gave a weak smile.

"Polite, too. Angwenth you could do wonders with a man like Grey!" She added in shaking her head.

"Mother! Injured, here." Angwenth growled, turning her head to hide a blush as Grey let out a soft chuckle.

"Right, right! Come in, come in." She moved out of the way before heading to the kitchen. "Tea?"

The kettle was already on the fire before Angwenth or Grey could protest. They followed her into the kitchen, each taking a seat at the wooden table sitting in the centre of the cheery room. Angwenth sunk into her own chair, placing Shadow on the ground. The dog barked and Mrs. Longbrair turned around. "And who is this little dear?"

"Shadow. My new pup." Angwenth said with a soft sigh. "His mother was killed by poachers."

Mrs. Longbrair nodded her head, not pushing any more. "I'll have your father go get the doctor then come back and start cleaning you two up."

She walked into another room as Grey glanced over at Angwenth. "This is what I mean for your home. Something a little more cheery, and feminine."

Angwenth rolled her eyes and glanced up at him. "I will hit you." She smiled though.

"We're together now, you can't hit me." Grey noted cheerfully.

"Watch me." Angwenth smirked.

Frowning he looked back at the door as Mrs. Longbrair came into the room. She began cleaning up any wounds and scrapes that Grey had, talking about random gossip around town as she did. Angwenth rested her head against the table as they spoke, hearing Grey barely muttering a response to her mother.

Chapter 5

She woke up, alone in the kitchen. Startled she jumped up, realizing she felt constricted. Looking down she noticed that her ribs were wrapped up, and she had a clean shirt on. There was talking from the living room. Angwenth got up to walk towards it. In a rocking chair sat her mother, knitting with some wool yarn. On the couch, with his feet curled under him sat Grey, who laughed at something Angwenth's father said. Angwenth's father sat on another chair, facing the fire.

Walking in she sat down on the opposite side of the couch from Grey. "How long was I out?"

"A few hours. The sun is setting soon." Mrs. Longbrair noted.

Angwenth wasn't sure how she looked away from the yarn and kept her count. The pieces always came out flawless, despite her mother's lack of attention.

"Shadow?" She asked sleepily, glancing around.

"Eating. He's in the other room with some food." Her mother said with a smile. "Such a cute thing."

Her father chimed in. "Yeah cute. Eating my steak."

With a smile Angwenth leaned back into the couch. "Thank you."

There was a silence, that only Angwenth didn't see as awkward. Her mother said softly. "So. You and Grey?"

Angwenth's eyes darted open, glancing at Grey. *He told them?* Grey shrugged. "Your mother is very convincing when she wants information."

Groaning, Angwenth reached up to rub the bridge of her nose. "Yes. Me and Grey."

She let out a cheerful sound, that she quickly muffled. The smile on her face didn't hide her excitement though. "That's so wonderful. I always said Grey was a wonderful man, didn't I dear?"

"Ya." was all her father added.

Angwenth groaned. "Can we talk about something else?"

Grey let out a chuckle but dropped the topic. Her father asked, his voice serious. "What happened?"

"Father, I said to drop it." Angwenth sighed.

"Not with you two. To cause the injuries." He added, his voice serious.

Angwenth knew that he would do whatever he could to protect her, despite the fact that she was almost as strong as he was.

She told them the events of the last few days, including how she came across Shadow, and the dog fights. She avoided going into details about the death, at least until they pushed her to share. As the details flashed through her mind, she shared. By the end she looked up, her father beamed with pride. "That's my girl! Killed all them men on your own."

"Not completely. The wolves helped." She added in.

Her mother smiled. "You thought of that though. That's very smart of you, dear."

Grey smiled at her. "Did better than if I would have been there. I would have gotten myself caught."

She laughed. Angwenth felt her ribs ache from it, but it felt good. "True. But you did help."

"How?" He asked seriously.

"You gave me someone to come back to."

It was Grey's turn to blush as he looked away. Shadow came bounding into the room, jumping onto the couch just in time to distract everyone. He rolled up on Angwenth's lap looking up at her as if to say 'What about me?'

"You, too, little buddy. Thanks for the assistance the first night, otherwise I'd be dead." She rubbed his head gently, and he laid his head on her lap to sleep.

***

Angwenth pushed open the carved wooden door without knocking. "I'm home."

The inside of the home was decorated in warm colours, more to match nature. Flowers were placed in pots and windows, which were open to let in as much light and sunshine as possible. Angwenth walked through the main room to the back where the kitchen was placed. In the kitchen, Grey stood at the counter chopping vegetables from the garden Angwenth had planted outside a year back. "Welcome home. How'd the hunting go?"

Shadow trotted up behind her. The pup was almost a full grown wolf, his nose at about the height of Angwenth's knee. His black fur, that had grown long and full, was caked in mud. He dropped the bundle in his mouth on the floor, letting his tongue hang out as it hit the floor in a splat. "Caught us some dinner."

He nodded and picked up the creature off the ground before going at it with a knife. "Go clean up. Dinner will be done soon."

Angwenth went to the washroom, while Shadow went outside to the small lake that was outside. They both came back clean, or at least less muddy, when Grey was placing dinner on the table. "Just in time." He frowned at the dirt but didn't make any comments.Sitting at the table they discussed each other's days. Angwenth had gone hunting with Shadow, spending most of the day outside. They managed to catch a few things, dropped some off to her parents before bring the rest home. Grey had stayed home most of the day, choosing the less dirty of the two options.

She had moved in a few months ago, after spending more time there then her own home. There was never a question as to whose house would be chosen when they decided to move in together. Grey's house had so much history and was much better built than her own. Angwenth's parents were thrilled, still counting down the days until grandchildren, despite Angwenth's reminder that she wanted to wait to have kids.

The forest had calmed down a lot in the last few months. There was never any mention outside of her parent's home about the dog fights, or the men in the forest. Lost pets found their way home, after only a few days of the incident, leaving many adults confused and children happy. Occasionally she heard rumours of someone finding bones or a burned corpse in the woods, though it was never linked back to anyone in particular. They kept it to themselves.

Angwenth had been working on her anger issues with Grey, though it wasn't coming along very well. Half the time she got mad of trying not to get mad, forcing herself to go calm down elsewhere. Grey was still beating off women with a stick, but true to his word, he never wavered in his faithfulness to Angwenth. A few of the women backed off when Angwenth began to growl at them. They thought she was crazy. She didn't mind though, and Grey always got a chuckle out of it.

Angwenth and Grey had talked about taken things the next step, but for now Angwenth threatened that if he ever tried to embarrass her she would kick his ass. He believed her, and kept his promise that if and when he proposed, it would be somewhere private. Mrs. Longbriar would stop by and drop not so subtle hints as to where the perfect place would be, but the smirk on his face gave away that Grey already knew where he would propose to her.

The place they had shared their first kiss. Their first hint of romance. Their home away from home

The End

About the Author

Nikki lives in Florida with her husband and eight pets. When she's not doing her day job she keeps herself busy with The Dragon's Rocketship, a Facebook group dedicated to those who love the world of fantasy and science fiction. During the last two years Nikki published a handful of anthologies, three of which included a short story written by her. The group went so well that in February 2016 The Dragon's Rocketship Publishing, LLC was born. She and her business partner, Mandi Yager, plan on publishing many books that fall under the genres of fantasy and science fiction and provide support to authors and writers who want to be published. In her limited free time she likes to read, write, draw, and play video games.

Acknowledgements

I would like to start by thanking Josh Vogt, Nikki Yager, Mary Hukel and Péter Holló-Vaskó for providing the fantastic stories.

Ali Jennings and Pete Sutton for editing the stories and providing feed back.

Ross D'Souza, Edward Morely for test reading the stories and providing some great constructive criticism.

I would like to thank Sandra and Stephen Beaumont for their help and support in getting the anthology completed

And last but not least a huge thank you to my wonderful fiancée

Donna Tindale, who has always been behind me and help support this project through what has been a turbulent journey.

It's been a wonderful journey and I feel that we have only begun to get started.

Craig Teal

Printed in Great Britain
by Amazon